The Happy Hollisters
and the
Cuckoo Clock Mystery

The Happy Hollisters and the Cuckoo Clock Mystery

BY JERRY WEST

Illustrated by Helen S. Hamilton

DOUBLEDAY & COMPANY, INC.
GARDEN CITY, NEW YORK

Contents

1	A BROKEN CUCKOO	1
2	A TURNABOUT TRICK	10
3	HUND UND KATZE	20
4	A DUPLICATE CLUE	30
5	A MERRY SONG	39
6	A WORD GAME	49
7	A REDHEADED ELF	58
8	THE OLD RUINS	70
9	A SHY BIRD	80
10	A SLIPPERY SLIDE	91
11	AN AMAZING CAT	103
12	THE SCHNITZELMEISTER	112
13	A WOODEN LION	120
14	A FRIENDLY DEER	128
15	THE CLOCK TOWER	140
16	UNLOCKING A RIDDLE	148
17	RICKY'S HUNCH	157
18	OLD TOWN TRAP	169

The Happy Hollisters
and the
Cuckoo Clock Mystery

CHAPTER 1

A Broken Cuckoo

"WHERE's the secret surprise, Daddy?" asked little Sue Hollister.

"Yes, you promised us," declared Holly. "We're all here to see it."

The five Hollister children had just trooped into The Trading Post, which was the combination hardware, sporting goods and toy store operated by their father in downtown Shoreham.

"Come right this way," said Mr. Hollister, a tall, athletic-looking man, as he led them to the rear of the store.

All of the children beamed in expectation as they followed. Dark-haired Sue, who was four, clung to her father's hand. Beside her was six-year-old Holly, twirling a pigtail. Red-haired Ricky came next. He was seven and had freckles. Pam and Pete brought up the rear. Pam, ten, had fluffy golden hair and a friendly smile. Pete, two years older, was a good-looking boy with a crew cut.

At the back of the store Mr. Hollister stopped and pointed to the wall. "There's the surprise!"

"Cuckoo clocks!" the youngsters chorused.

Everyone gazed at the three clocks mounted high

on the wall. The wooden faces of the clocks were framed with hand-carved leaves, and on the peaked roof of each was a lovely bird with wings outstretched. Beneath, dangling nearly to the floor, were two long chains, weighted by pine cones made of metal.

The time was one minute to ten. "Watch carefully," Mr. Hollister said.

Suddenly the doors of the cuckoo clocks sprang open and three little birds poked their heads out.

"*Cuckoo! Cuckoo! Cuckoo!*" they called, accompanied by the jangling sounds of gongs.

Sue clapped her hands gleefully and Pam said, "Oh, they're precious!"

But on the ninth *cuckoo* there came a loud *bang!* as a small stone smashed against a clock and fell to the floor at their feet.

"Oh dear!" exclaimed Pam.

The middle cuckoo hung limply forward while the other two disappeared into their birdhouses. The Hollisters wheeled about to see Joey Brill dashing toward the front door of The Trading Post. In one hand he held a slingshot.

"He shot the cuckoo!" Holly cried out.

"Come on, Pete! We'll get him!" Ricky said stoutly.

The two boys raced down the aisle and outside. Joey Brill was nowhere to be seen.

"That was a mean trick!" Pete said in disgust as

"He shot the cuckoo!" Holly cried out.

the two boys gave up their search and returned to their father's store.

Inside, Mr. Hollister had lifted the damaged clock from the wall and placed it on top of the counter. "I saw Joey here earlier this morning," Mr. Hollister said. "He was looking at the cuckoo clocks, but I never thought he'd do this."

"The meanie!" Pam declared.

"Yes, it's too bad." Her father frowned. "These clocks came all the way from Germany."

"Will we have to send this one back for repairs?" Pete asked.

"No. I think we can fix it here," Mr. Hollister replied. He tried to push the cuckoo back into its house, but the poor bird said "Coo" in a mournful tone and refused to budge.

"Look!" Ricky pointed. "The door is cracked, Daddy. That's the reason."

"So it is," his father said. "And the wire which holds it open is bent, too."

Pam noticed that the door was made of two pieces of wood, which had been sealed face to face. "I'll get some glue," she offered.

Pete, meanwhile, took a knife from his pocket and separated the two flat squares of wood so that Pam might insert the glue. In doing so, he noticed a small white paper between the two faces of the little door.

"Hey, look at this!" Pete exclaimed as he carefully pried out the paper.

4

"There's writing on it!" Holly observed.

Pam had now returned with a tube of glue. When she saw the white paper spread open, she said, "I think that's written in German."

"You're right," Mr. Hollister agreed.

"Do you suppose it's instructions for the cuckoo clock?" Pete asked.

"I think not," his father replied. "This message is handwritten." While the others examined the strange note, Pete took the glue and repaired the broken door.

Mr. Hollister now straightened the wire and the little bird popped back into the clock. Ricky and Sue, meanwhile, had looked about and found a round stone on the floor.

"This is what Joey shot the poor cuckoo with," Sue said.

"Well, luckily there's not too much damage done," Mr. Hollister remarked cheerfully.

"But what about the message?" Pete asked.

"If it *is* a message," Pam said, laughing.

"Who knows any German?" Ricky asked as he watched his father replace the cuckoo clock on the back wall of the store.

Pete suggested Otto Elser, a German butcher who had a shop nearby.

"That's a good idea," Mr. Hollister said, "but I'd like to ask a favor of you two boys." He glanced toward the front of the store, where several customers had entered.

5

"You want us to be salesmen?" Pete asked.

"We'd be glad to," Ricky said importantly.

"Then we girls will visit Mr. Elser," Pam decided. Carefully she folded the paper and put it in the pocket of her dress. "Maybe there is a mystery in this note."

Hand in hand, Pam, Holly and Sue walked down the street to Mr. Elser's place. The butcher was a stout, jolly man with a mustache. Because he was short, he stood on a platform behind the counter, which made him look much taller.

"Hello, girls," he said with a heavy accent as the children walked in. "What would you like?"

"Can you read German?" Holly spoke up eagerly.

"*Jawohl, jawohl*. Better can I read German than English," the butcher said with a chuckle. "Big words in German I know, but in English—" He shook his head, picked up a long knife and began to sharpen it.

"We would like you to do us a favor, please," Pam said to him shyly.

"I know. You would like some of my homemade knockwurst, *ja?*"

"Not today," Pam replied with a giggle. "We have a note in German we want you to translate for us."

"In German? *Jawohl*," the butcher said, and wiped his hands on his white apron.

"What does *jawohl* mean?" Sue piped up.

6

The butcher chuckled. "It means yes indeed, and I will translate your note. *Jawohl.*"

Pam reached up over the high counter to hand the paper to Mr. Elser. He examined it carefully. As he looked up, he glanced over the heads of the girls at something outside the window.

"Hmm," Mr. Elser said, frowning. He read more of the note and glanced toward the street again. The three sisters kept their eyes on the butcher's face all the time.

"Does it say something important?" Holly asked.

"Maybe yes, maybe no," Mr. Elser said mysteriously. He put the note on his scales, reached inside the refrigerator case and pulled out a chunk of Swiss cheese. He cut three slices and handed them to the girls.

"Thank you," they said and Pam added, "Have you translated the message already, Mr. Elser?"

The butcher looked out the window again and gave a grunt.

Holly's eyes roved to a tub of dill pickles beside the counter. She said nothing but licked her lips.

"Yes, I have translated it," the butcher said finally. He picked up the note and read:

"Three o'clock to the waterfall.
Six o'clock to the chimney pot.
Nine o'clock to the wooden stair.
Twelve o'clock to the golden cuckoo."

"What does that mean?" Pam asked, perplexed.

"It's a mystery of some kind," the butcher answered, "—in Germany."

Pam repeated what Mr. Elser had translated until she had it firmly memorized. "Thank you so much," she said.

"*Jawohl*," the butcher replied. "Wait a minute. I'll give you an envelope."

Taking the note, he stepped down from his platform and walked away. He reappeared a few moments later with an envelope, which he handed to Pam. "This way your message is safe," he said.

The three girls thanked him and hurried from the shop, eager to return to Pete and Ricky. But only two doors from Mr. Elser's place they were confronted by Joey Brill and his friend Will Wilson. Joey was as old as Pete, but heavier. He usually wore a scowl on his face and this day was no exception. Will Wilson, who always followed Joey around, spoke up first.

"We saw you in the butcher shop," he said loudly. "Why didn't you buy something?"

Pam held her chin high and began to walk past.

"Ha, ha!" Joey jeered. "You're mad because we shot your old cuckoo!"

Pam faced him squarely. "You are mean to destroy other people's property," she said. "You'd better not let Pete get hold of you!"

"Aw, who's afraid of him?" Will retorted.

"What do you have in that envelope?" Joey demanded. "We saw you show a note to Mr. Elser."

"We have a new mystery!" Sue blurted out.

"I'll bet!" Joey scoffed.

"It's about Germany," Holly said importantly.

As Pam started to walk on, Will taunted, "A mystery in Germany—that's rich!"

"It's not so!" Joey declared.

"It is too so!" Holly retorted. "Show him the note, Pam."

"Yeah, let's see it," Joey said. "I'll give it back to you, honest."

Before Pam could say yes or no, the boy flicked the envelope from her hand. He turned away, opened it and read the paper inside.

"Oh," he remarked knowingly, "that's interesting."

"What do you know about that?" said Will, who looked over his shoulder. After a moment Joey turned around and handed the envelope back to Pam. "See, I told you I'd give it back," he said.

The two bullies walked on and the girls hastened to The Trading Post.

"Ricky! Pete!" Pam called out. "We have found another mystery!"

"Crickets!" Pete exclaimed. "What's it about?"

"We don't know, really," Pam replied, and she repeated the German butcher's translation.

"Let me see that message again," Pete said, taking the envelope.

He opened it and looked inside. The mysterious note was gone!

CHAPTER 2

A Turnabout Trick

PETE turned the envelope upside down and shook it, but the mysterious message was gone.

"Now Joey has the key to the riddle," Pam said, crestfallen, and told about meeting the bullies.

Tears came to Holly's eyes. "Oh, I shouldn't have told him about our new mystery!" she wailed.

"Neither should I," sniffled Sue.

Pete said that Joey or Will must have palmed the message, making it look as if they had put the paper back into the envelope.

"It's a good thing I memorized the translation which Mr. Elser gave us," Pam remarked.

"Things could be worse, I guess," Pete agreed. "But it's too bad Joey and Will are in on our mystery."

"Do you think they may be able to solve it before we do?" Ricky asked anxiously.

"It's possible," the older boy admitted. "But we're going to do our best to prevent it. Pam, you and I'll track down Joey and Will and get that paper back."

Just then Mrs. Hollister walked into The Trading Post. The pretty, slender, blonde-haired woman had been shopping and offered to drive Ricky, Holly and Sue home with her.

"Good luck with Joey and Will!" Ricky called back as he followed his mother and sisters out of the store.

The older pair set out immediately, walking about downtown Shoreham in an effort to find the note snatchers. The bullies were nowhere in sight.

"They'll probably try to get the message translated," Pam said.

"Yes," Pete agreed, "but by whom? I don't think they'd dare take it to Mr. Elser."

As the children turned a corner Pam suddenly stopped her brother. "Look! I just saw them go into the Soda Shoppe!"

Pete and Pam hurried to the door of the popular sweetshop and peeked inside. Joey and Will were seated on stools before the counter, whispering together. Just then a group of students, who were attending summer classes at Shoreham High School, entered, laughing and joking. Pete and Pam walked in with them and, unnoticed, slid into a booth directly behind Joey and Will.

The Hollisters watched intently as the boys at the counter ordered ice cream. When they were served, Joey leaned forward and asked the clerk, "Can you read German?"

The soda man tilted his white hat over his forehead and examined the paper that Joey gave him.

"Do I look like a professor?" he asked with a laugh and handed the note back. "Sorry."

Pete and Pam smiled with relief.

"How shall we get it away from them?" the girl asked softly as Joey and Will studied the paper, holding it right side up and upside down. Just then a waiter came to the Hollisters' booth. He was a customer at The Trading Post and knew them.

"Hi, Pete. Hello, Pam," he said. "What'll you have today?"

Instantly Joey and Will swung around on their stools and glared.

"So! You're spying on us!" Joey blustered.

Pete rose from his seat. "Give us back that note!" he demanded, going over to the bullies.

"What note?" Will asked with mock innocence.

"The one you snitched from us," Pete replied. "We heard you ask for a translation."

Pam joined her brother. "Yes, you just put it in your pocket, Joey. I saw you."

The soda man leaned over the counter. "See here! No arguments!" he said sternly. Then he looked at Joey. "Maybe one of the high school teachers can translate that note for you."

The boy's face flushed with embarrassment. Without another word he and Will leaped off the stools and hurried out of the store.

"Oh, I'd like to punch him in the nose," Pete said, "for meddling in our mystery!"

Pam sighed. "The worst part is, they still have the note."

She and Pete followed the pair, being careful to conceal themselves in doorways or behind trees.

"Look!" Pete said. "They're going toward the high school."

"They'll get that message translated yet," Pam said. "This is not our day for luck, Pete!"

As Joey and Will approached the front entrance, several women teachers descended the stone steps. Joey walked up to one of them.

Pete and Pam saw Joey hand the woman the white paper and ask her a question. She nodded, looked at the note for a moment, then said something and laughed. Joey and Will hurried off.

"That does it!" Pete said. "Now they know our secret."

"But they haven't solved the mystery yet," Pam said, trying to console her downcast brother.

As the Hollisters made their way home, Pam repeated Mr. Elser's translation over and over for Pete, so that he had learned it by the time they arrived at their home on the shore of Pine Lake.

The Hollisters' large, rambling house lay between the road and the water's edge. It was set amid broad lawns and shady trees.

Pete and Pam had hardly reached the end of their driveway when Ricky, Holly and Sue, who had been playing on the Hollisters' dock, raced up.

"Did you get the note back?" Ricky asked breathlessly.

Pete shook his head. "We have bad news," he said as they trooped into the house.

The children found their mother putting sandwiches and lemonade on the kitchen table. While they all ate lunch, Pete and Pam told their story. When it was finished, Mrs. Hollister looked at the circle of glum faces.

"Let's think of a special dessert," she said. "That'll cheer you up."

Just then a horn tooted in the driveway. Holly went to the window.

"It's Mr. Elser," she exclaimed.

The children hurried outside to greet the butcher, who was just alighting from his delivery truck.

"Hello, Mr. Elser," Pam said. "Guess what happened to us!"

"It was a mean trick, too!" Holly chimed in.

"He's a bad, bad boy!" Sue declared.

"Wait a minute," Pete interrupted. "I'll bet Mr. Elser doesn't even know what we're talking about."

"*Jawohl,*" the butcher said wisely, bobbing his head. "I know all about it."

"How?" Pam asked in amazement.

The butcher explained that he had seen Joey and Will lurking outside his store.

"Oh, dear!" said Pam, "I wish you'd told us."

"Yes," Pete added. "They got hold of our secret message and had it translated."

14

A broad smile came over Mr. Elser's round face and his mustache twitched with mirth.

"Yikes! It isn't funny!" Ricky exclaimed.

"*Ja*, it is funny!" Mr. Elser said as his round middle began to shake with laughter. When he had finished chuckling, the butcher reached into his pocket and pulled out a piece of white paper. He handed it to Pam.

"Here," he said, "this is the real note. I put another one in the envelope you took away. I thought maybe those pests, Joey and Will, might take it from you."

Looks of disbelief on the faces of the five Hollisters quickly turned to grins.

"What did you put in the envelope, Mr. Elser?" Pete asked.

The butcher's eyebrows arched and he began to chuckle again. "Mrs. Meyer's shopping list," he answered.

"Written in German?" Pam queried.

"*Ja*, Mrs. Meyer writes best in German," the butcher explained. "The words on that paper said, 'Dear Mr. Elser: Please send me two pounds of knockwurst with sauerkraut.'"

The children burst out laughing and Ricky hooted with glee. He gave three handsprings, landing flat on his back in the soft grass. The joke was on the bullies!

"*Ja*, if there is a German mystery," Mr. Elser went on, "I would like only the Hollisters to solve

The joke was on the bullies!

it. Maybe my cousin, Gerhart Elser, could help you. He is captain of a big boat on the Rhine River. It is named the *Eureka*."

Then the jolly man reached into the truck, pulled out a package and gave it to Pam. "Something for you children," he said. With that he climbed behind the wheel and drove off.

Pam unwrapped the package carefully. The paper was damp. When she finally had it opened, there were five fat dill pickles.

"Oh, yummy!" Holly exclaimed. "Here's our special dessert!" The children ran into the house munching on their sour treat.

Holly gave her mother a couple of bites while Pam told the story of the fake message.

Mrs. Hollister's eyes twinkled. "I'd say the tables are really turned."

Sue looked perplexed and eyed the kitchen table. "They are?"

Pam smiled. "Mother means Joey and Will fooled us—and now they've been fooled."

When the children had finished eating and washed their hands, a knock came on the front door. There, framed in the screen, was the tall figure of a man. "May I come in?" he asked.

"Uncle Russ!" the youngsters chorused.

"Goodness! What a surprise!" Mrs. Hollister said. "But how nice to see you!"

As the good-looking man came into the living room, his nieces and nephews swarmed over him.

Russ Hollister was their father's younger brother. He was a newspaper cartoonist, and lived with his wife and two children in the town of Crestwood.

"I was driving along the turnpike toward New York," Uncle Russ said, "so I thought I'd stop in and stay overnight."

The Hollister children played with their favorite uncle all afternoon and kept plying him with questions about Crestwood, where they used to live, and about their cousins Teddy and Jean.

When the family was at the dinner table that evening, Pete asked, "Uncle Russ, how is Mr. Spencer, that nice man who helped us solve the secret of the lucky coins?"

"He's fine," came the reply. "And," Uncle Russ added, narrowing an eye mysteriously, "he's part of the reason for my visit here."

"Does he have another mystery?" Ricky asked.

"Something like that," the cartoonist replied.

"Oh, please tell us!" Holly begged.

Uncle Russ said that there had been a fire in Mr. Spencer's home and that a lion had been destroyed.

"Oh, dear!" Pam exclaimed. "I didn't know he had a—a lion!"

"A wooden one, that is," her uncle explained, grinning. "Years ago," he continued, "Mr. Spencer's father brought a large, carved wooden lion from Germany. He prized it highly, for it had been made by a famous *Schnitzelmeister*."

"A *Schnitzel* what?" Pete asked.

Mr. Hollister explained that a *Schnitzelmeister* was a German wood-carving master. "There aren't many of them left," he told the children.

"That's right, John," Uncle Russ agreed and added, "Mr. Spencer would like another lion."

"A full-sized one?" asked Ricky, putting down his forkful of chocolate cake.

"Not quite," his uncle replied with a chuckle. "Just about as large as Zip." He motioned to the Hollisters' beautiful big collie dog, who lay on the rug in the living room watching them.

"But—but how can we help Mr. Spencer find a new lion?" Pam asked.

For a moment Uncle Russ seemed surprised. Then he said, "On your trip to Germany."

The Hollister children looked stunned. They glanced from one to the other.

"Going to *Germany!*" Pete blurted. "What do you mean, Uncle Russ?"

The cartoonist winced and closed his eyes.

Mr. Hollister grinned, leaned over and thumped his brother on the arm. "Russ!" he declared. "You've let the cat out of the bag!"

CHAPTER 3

Hund und Katze

"ARE we really going to Germany!" Pete exploded.

"Why didn't you tell us, Mother?" Pam asked, hardly able to believe the good news.

Mrs. Hollister explained that she and her husband had not definitely made up their minds until several days before. "We were going to surprise you tomorrow," she told them.

"And I had to spoil it!" Uncle Russ said regretfully.

"But—but I don't see the cat you let out of the bag," Sue remarked, glancing about the dining room.

"That means he told a secret before he should have," Holly said, giggling.

Questions, answers and happy remarks flew back and forth across the table as the Hollisters bubbled delightedly over the prospect of a trip to Germany.

"Now we can solve the mystery of the strange message," Pam said.

"Provided we're able to pick up the trail," Pete added.

"And you might find an expert wood carver too," Uncle Russ reminded them.

"Lions and cuckoos!" Mrs. Hollister declared gaily. "What an adventure we will have!"

"If we find an old *Schnitzelmeister*," Ricky said, "maybe he can teach us how to carve little birds and animals and things."

Their uncle suggested that they might start practicing right away. "Soap carving would be a good way to learn," he suggested.

"Will you show us, please?" Holly begged. "After we help Mother clear the dishes, that is."

When the kitchen chores had been completed, Mrs. Hollister provided cakes of soap and some small knives which were sharp enough, but not dangerous for the children to use. Pam spread newspapers on the kitchen table, and they all sat down to receive instructions from their uncle.

First the cartoonist drew a little figure on each cake of soap.

"Oh, look! Mine's a duck," Sue declared.

"I have a dog," Holly said.

"Mine's a goat," Ricky remarked proudly.

Their uncle sketched a boy and a girl for Pete and Pam. Then he showed the children how to cut away the soap in tiny bits.

"Be sure to follow the outline," he cautioned, "and don't cut too deeply, or you might break the soap."

Sue worked on her duck until she began to yawn.

"Oh, look! Mine's a duck," Sue declared.

When the little girl's eyelids drooped, Pam took her by the hand. "It's time for bed, honey," she said.

"Don't let my duck swim away," Sue said drowsily as she was led upstairs. Mrs. Hollister followed to put her youngest child to bed, and Pam returned to her carving.

She and Pete finished their projects first and were praised by their uncle.

"I think you would make good wood carvers," he said.

"But I'd rather play detective," Pete confided as he and his sister went into the living room to talk over vacation plans with their parents. Holly and Ricky remained behind, working with Uncle Russ.

"Why did you pick Germany for our trip, Dad?" Pete asked as he plopped onto the sofa.

His father explained that they would go to many places in Europe, but Germany was first on his schedule because he had to buy some toys for The Trading Post.

"And Christmas window decorations too," Mrs. Hollister added.

Pete and Pam learned that they would fly from New York to Frankfurt, and then travel wherever they pleased.

"You mean we'll have time to follow cuckoo clock clues?" Pete asked.

"Yes, if you find any good ones," came Mr. Hollister's reply.

"Something will have to be done about our pets,"

Mrs. Hollister reminded them. "They can't go along."

"I'm sure that Dave Mead would take care of Zip," Pete declared.

Pam said that Donna Martin was waiting for an opportunity to care for White Nose and her kittens.

"And Domingo will stay right in his stall in the garage," Mr. Hollister said. "Indy Roades will feed him."

"And ride him once in a while," Pam added with a grin.

Domingo was the pet burro the Hollisters had received as a gift. Indy Roades, a real Indian from New Mexico, worked at The Trading Post and was very fond of the black donkey.

"We'll talk to Dave and Donna first thing in the morning," Pete said.

By bedtime all the little soap figures had been cut out and Uncle Russ had put the finishing touches on Sue's duck. Then the chips were gathered up for Mrs. Hollister to use in her washing machine, and the family went to bed.

After breakfast next morning, Holly went into the basement to give milk and cat food to White Nose and her five kittens, Tutti-Frutti, Cuddly, Snowball, Midnight and Smoky.

The furry creatures were scampering about the comfortable quilt-lined box where they lived, but when they saw Holly set down the saucers of milk, they minced forward with tails erect and began to lap up the cool liquid. Holly giggled when she saw the tiny drops of milk on the cats' whiskers.

"Come on, Cuddly," she said, picking up one of the little pets and holding it over her arm like a purse. "We're going to visit Donna Martin."

Pam and Sue joined Holly, and as they skipped out of the front yard, they saw Pete running toward Dave Mead's house a few doors down the street. Zip was bounding along at his heels. Pete found his friend cutting the lawn with a power mower.

"Hi!" called Dave, and turned off the noisy machine.

Dave was a pleasant dark-haired boy and Pete's best friend. "You look excited," he said. "Have you discovered another mystery?"

"You guessed it," Pete said, and leaned down to scratch the ruff on the collie's neck. "You know what else, Dave? We're all going to Germany!"

"To solve the mystery?"

"That's part of it. Would you like to take care of Zip?"

"That would be keen! How long are you going to be away?"

"I don't know exactly. Three or four weeks, maybe."

"My mother and dad spent some time in Germany," Dave told him.

"Really? Maybe your mother can answer some questions for me," Pete said.

"Sure. Come on in. She's making pies in the kitchen."

The two boys hurried inside Dave's house and pulled up chairs to watch Mrs. Mead flatten a batch of dough with a rolling pin.

"I understand you were once in Germany," Pete said to her. "Did you see any cuckoo clocks over there?"

"Yes indeed," declared Mrs. Mead, a short, dark-haired, brisk-moving woman. "Cuckoo clocks are made in the *Schwarzwald*. *Schwarz* means black," she explained, "and *Wald* is the word for forest."

"Black Forest," Pete remarked. "Sounds like a spooky place."

"Not really," Mrs. Mead went on as she picked up a circle of dough and laid it in a pie tin. "Most of the cuckoo clocks are made in a little town called Triberg."

She said that the village lay in a steep valley and added, with a chuckle, "You have to walk either up- or downhill."

After Pete had told her about their plans for boarding the pets, Dave's mother piled a dish of sliced apples into the pie tin and said, "The German word for dog is *Hund*. A cat is called *die Katze*."

"*Hund und Katze*," Pete said. "I must remember that."

"If you want to say mister," the woman continued, "the word is *Herr*. Mrs. is *Frau*."

The boys watched with interest as Mrs. Mead

26

flipped a cover of dough over the top of the piepan, scalloped the edges with her fingers, cut slits in the top, sprinkled the dough with sugar and put the tin in the oven.

No sooner had she closed the door when the sound of anguished cries came from outside. Dave and Pete dashed to the front door to see Pam, Sue and Holly running down the street. Pam had Cuddly clutched tightly in her arms. Joey Brill was in hot pursuit.

"Let them alone!" Pete shouted as he and Dave raced to the rescue of the three girls.

Joey backed off and held up his fists. "If you want to fight, come on!" he challenged.

"He was going to skin Cuddly!" Holly cried heatedly.

"Oh, who wants to skin an old kitten!" Joey said disdainfully. "There wouldn't be enough fur to make even one ear muff."

"I thought you were busy with Will Wilson," Pete declared. "We understood you two fellows were solving the knockwurst mystery."

Joey glared at them. "You tricked us," he stormed. "I don't know how. But I'll get even with you!"

"Not by skinning our cat," Pete said with a chuckle.

Joey ran off shaking his fist.

"So long, Sauerkraut," Ricky called.

"Well, he won't be bothering us much longer,"

Pam said with a sigh of relief, "because we'll be in Germany."

The Hollisters returned home for lunch with Uncle Russ. Shortly afterward he made ready to leave, wishing them all a happy trip to Europe. "And I hope you solve the cuckoo clock mystery."

"We'll try," Pam promised.

"And get the lion, too," Holly declared after she kissed her uncle good-by.

The rest of the afternoon was taken up with preparations for the big journey.

When suppertime came, the children washed their hands before going to the table. Sue came out of the bathroom with tears rolling down her cheeks.

"What's the matter?" Mrs. Hollister asked her small daughter.

"I used my soap duck," she said, "and now it doesn't have any head."

"Oh, don't worry," Pam consoled her. "You may have my soap girl. I can make another one."

After supper was over, Pete schooled his brother and sisters in the new German words he had learned, and told his parents about Triberg and the Black Forest.

"Daddy, do you suppose that's where our cuckoo clocks came from?" Pam asked.

Mr. Hollister replied that he did not remember. "But the bill is in our office files," he said. "Perhaps you can look at it tomorrow."

"Tonight, please, Daddy," Pam said. "It may be a clue for us."

"Crickets! That's a good idea," Pete said. "I know where your filing cabinet is, Dad. May Pam and I go down to The Trading Post?"

Their father agreed and gave Pete a key to his store.

"I'll drive you down," Mrs. Hollister offered.

"Thank you, Mother," Pam said and gave her a hug.

It was nearly dark when the three arrived at The Trading Post. As Mrs. Hollister was parking, Pete noticed someone moving at the end of the alley next to the store.

"Mother," he exclaimed, "someone's prowling around our place!"

The trio got out of the car, walked cautiously down the alley and peered around the corner.

In the darkness they could make out two figures stooping before the lock on the back door.

"Who are you? What do you want?" Mrs. Hollister demanded.

Startled, the intruders fled down the narrow lane behind The Trading Post.

"Stop!" Pete shouted as the Hollisters raced after them.

A Duplicate Clue

THE two fugitives darted past the adjoining store and down the next alley, with Pete leading the pursuit. Reaching the sidewalk, the boy saw a car speed away from the curb. He ran after it, but the red taillights swiftly disappeared around a corner.

Pete was quickly joined by Pam and Mrs. Hollister.

"They got away before I could catch the license number," Pete told them. "I'm going to call the police," he added and dashed down the street to an outside phone booth. He dialed headquarters and spoke to the desk lieutenant.

"Your friend Officer Cal is here," the man said. "We'll dispatch him immediately."

Pete walked back to his mother and sister at The Trading Post and a few minutes later Officer Cal Newberry drove up in a prowl car. He was a sandy-haired, handsome young man who had helped the Hollisters in several of their mysteries. After an exchange of greetings, Pete led Cal to the rear of the store and showed him the lock the intruders had tried to open.

"We couldn't see them very well because it was almost dark," Mrs. Hollister said.

"They were short fellows," Pete added.

"Well, first thing is to search the premises for clues," Cal said.

He beamed a powerful flashlight over the ground, looking for evidence which the prowlers might have left. But after circling The Trading Post and the adjacent store three times, he and the Hollisters had found nothing.

"There's one place we haven't looked yet," Pete said and told Cal about the car he had seen.

The boy led the way to the street and looked along the outer edge of the sidewalk.

"Crickets! What's this!" Pete exclaimed, picking up a piece of paper in the street about two feet from the curb. Cal flashed his light on it.

"That's a carbon copy of a bill," Mrs. Hollister observed.

"Look! Our name is on it!" Pam said excitedly.

"And it's from Germany," Cal added. "Does that mean anything to you?"

"I'll say!" Pete declared and scrutinized the duplicate bill more carefully.

At the top was the Hollisters' name and address with the initials U.S.A. under the word Shoreham. The name of the company stood out boldly: Karl Fritz, Kuckucksuhrenfabrikation, Triberg, Schwarzwald.

"Crickets! What's this?" Pete exclaimed.

"Crickets! It could have been dropped by one of the men as he escaped in the car!" Pete said.

He and Pam quickly told Officer Cal about the cuckoo clock mystery.

"I'd say these fellows are after one or all of the clocks," Officer Cal declared.

"Let's look at the files in the store right away," Pam urged. "I'm sure this paper is a duplicate of the one sent to Daddy."

Using the key that Mr. Hollister had given them, Pete unlocked the front door and they entered The Trading Post. Pam switched on the lights and the four made their way into the office, which contained several filing cabinets.

"Here's the one that holds the bills and orders," Mrs. Hollister said.

Quickly Pam pulled out a drawer and looked under the heading Cuckoo Clocks. In one folder she found the bill which had come with the shipment from Germany.

"Oh!" Pam said as she pulled out a piece of white paper. "It *is* the same! That was a duplicate bill you found, Pete."

Officer Cal wondered how the copy came to be in America.

"I'll bet the prowlers got our address from this," Pete said, turning it over to the policeman.

Pam had the mysterious note in the pocket of her dress and showed it to their friend, telling him of its translation.

Officer Cal whistled. "No doubt you have found a very important message," he said, "and since you are all going to Germany, perhaps you can return it to this man named Karl Fritz."

"Maybe he put the note in the clock himself," Pam suggested, "and now he wants it back."

"Do you think he might have sent these two men to get it?" Pete asked.

"No," replied Officer Cal, shaking his head. He reasoned that if Mr. Fritz had wanted a particular cuckoo clock back, he could have written to The Trading Post with his request. "It would have been a simple matter," the policeman added, "to send you a whole new shipment of clocks in return for the original ones."

"Then someone else besides Mr. Fritz wants that note," Pete said.

"And he'll stoop to thievery to get it," the policeman added as Pam replaced the original bill and closed the file. Pete turned off the lights then, and they left The Trading Post.

Before driving off the policeman called out, "I'll send a man over here to stand guard just in case the prowlers return."

Next morning Officer Cal telephoned the Hollisters to report that the intruders had not come back.

"But I'll keep my eyes open," the policeman promised, "and there'll be a man stationed at the store every night." After wishing his young friends *bon voyage,* he hung up.

The children speculated about the two prowlers and the strange clue they had dropped, but they had not much time to think about the mystery.

During the next two days, preparations for the family's flight overseas were in full swing. Donna Martin had taken White Nose and her kittens after Sue had kissed them each good-by; Dave Mead had built a doghouse especially for Zip's visit; and in the various bedrooms of the Hollister home suitcases were being packed.

"Dad," Pam said the night before their flight, "I'm going to take the original German message with me. If Mr. Fritz didn't write it himself, he might be able to tell who did."

"Good idea," her father replied.

"Let's take the cuckoo clock, too," Pete put in. "Perhaps Mr. Fritz will be able to see a clue in it that we can't."

Mr. Hollister thought this was a possibility, so Pete packed the wooden clock in a strong carton, which he wrapped tightly with white cord. Then he printed his name, address and "Contents: Cuckoo Clock" on the box.

Next morning was Sunday and the family attended church. In the afternoon Indy Roades drove them to the local airport.

As the Hollisters boarded the plane, Holly cried merrily, "Good-by, good-by to Shoreham!"

Several hours later they landed at International Airport, New York, to await the giant plane that would carry them over the Atlantic Ocean to Frankfurt, Germany.

"My goodness!" Mrs. Hollister said as they came down the steps of the aircraft. "This is a gigantic place. It looks like an entire city!"

Sounds of happy people arriving and departing mingled with the roar of jet engines as the great silver birds soared into the sky.

When the Hollisters entered the high, vaulted departure building, Pam took Sue and Holly by the hand. "Stay close to us," she said, "because you might get lost. And Ricky, hold on tightly to the cuckoo clock."

"Don't worry," replied her brother, twining his fingers more securely through the stout cord on the box.

The family followed a porter who took their other baggage in a hand truck to the airport counter. There it was weighed by an attendant and the children watched, fascinated, as each piece was put on a moving platform and disappeared through an opening in the wall behind the counter.

"Will we ever get them back again?" Sue wondered aloud. Pete assured her that the baggage would be returned to them on their arrival in Frankfurt.

After checking the Hollisters' tickets, the attendant gave them their seat numbers for the airplane.

Then the family settled down on a long bench where passengers were waiting for their flights.

Holly sat on the edge of the seat, kicking her feet and gazing out pensively.

"Penny for your thoughts, honey," Pam said.

"I was thinking," Holly replied, "that now we are natives. Tomorrow we'll all be foreigners."

Her mother's chuckle was interrupted by a voice which filled the huge room. "Will Mr. John Hollister please come to the telephone at the airline ticket counter?"

Startled looks crossed the faces of the five children. What could have happened?

"Wait here," their father said. "I'll be right back."

As Mr. Hollister strode across the room, Ricky spied a fountain on the other side. "Mother, may I get a drink while Daddy is gone?" he asked.

His mother nodded and Ricky, still holding onto the cuckoo clock, scurried across the polished floor toward the fountain.

His father, meanwhile, took the phone at the ticket counter and spoke for a few minutes. His face looked serious as he returned to the others.

"Oh, there's been trouble!" Mrs. Hollister guessed.

"I'm afraid there has, Elaine," came the reply. "That was Indy. He says that someone stole the other two cuckoo clocks from our store while he was bringing us to the airport."

"Oh, how awful!" Pam wailed.

"The police are guarding the place only at night," Mr. Hollister said.

"Crickets! Those two men again!" was Pete's guess. "This mystery is really getting exciting, Dad."

"That message you children found must be of greater importance than anyone realizes," Mr. Hollister said. He glanced about. "Where's Ricky?"

"He went for a drink," Pete replied, looking across the waiting room.

"Here he comes now," Holly said. Then she gasped. "He doesn't have the box!"

Ricky ran toward them, looking as if he were about to burst out crying. "It's gone!"

"What happened?" his father asked as Ricky wrung his hands nervously.

"I put the cuckoo clock down so I could get a drink," the boy said, "and when I turned around it wasn't there."

CHAPTER 5

A Merry Song

"I'M sorry I lost the cuckoo clock," Ricky said, hanging his head.

"You didn't lose it," Pam told him. "It was stolen from you."

Their father sighed. "We probably are being followed by one of the thieves."

"We ought to tell the airport police about this," Pete declared.

"There isn't time," Mr. Hollister replied, checking his watch. "In five minutes the call will come to board the plane."

"The thief might have known where the message was hidden," Pam said. "Maybe he tore off the door and threw the clock away. He would attract less attention without it."

"Perhaps it's in a trash basket," Holly suggested.

"If only we could find the clock," Pete added, "it might give us a clue to the thief."

"Please, Daddy," Pam urged, "let us search for five minutes."

"We promise to come right back as soon as we hear the boarding call," Pete put in.

As Ricky and Holly added their pleas, Mr. Hollister consented.

"But Sue will stay here," Mrs. Hollister said. "Losing a cuckoo clock is bad enough. I wouldn't want this little cricket to get away from us."

The four children hurried off. Darting in and out of the crowd, they looked into each trash receptacle. No cuckoo clock.

Pete excitedly fished out a small brown carton, without any luck.

"Maybe there was something else valuable in the clock," Ricky ventured, "and the crook kept the whole thing."

Minutes had passed and the children had gone so far down the huge room that Pam said worriedly that they had better turn back.

As she spoke, Pete spotted another waste container.

"*Look!*" he said, "there's a white string hanging down the side!" The children hurried over and peered into the tall can.

"It's here!" Pete exclaimed, pulling out the carton with the crumpled paper and string.

Inside was the clock. As Pam had expected, the little door had been torn off. The birdhouse was empty and the cuckoo lay loose in the box.

Just then came the voice of the public address announcer: "Flight 701 boarding at gate 14. Nonstop flight to Frankfurt!"

"That's us!" Holly cried.

Clutching the box, Pete hurried through the crowd with the others close behind him.

"We found it!" Ricky said as the four youngsters reached their mother and father. Before either parent could answer, the boarding call was repeated.

The booming announcement sent thrills through the young passengers.

"Just think," Pam said, as they walked into a long movable tunnel that led right to the door of the airplane, "we're going to fly all the way across the Atlantic Ocean."

Mrs. Hollister led the way down the aisle of the huge craft. The five children followed, and their father brought up the rear. The hushed atmosphere and the quiet, cheerful voices of the three stewardesses made Pam feel that they were in another world. Passengers moved almost silently to find their seats.

"Here are our places," Pam said. She sat between Ricky and Holly, while their parents and Sue occupied the three seats in front of them. As Pete found his place on the aisle across from Holly, he noticed several empty seats nearby. Obeying a lighted sign, the children fastened their safety belts.

Suddenly a stout man came rushing up the aisle and plopped, panting, into the seat behind Holly. The stewardess paused beside him and said, smiling, "We're glad you made it aboard, sir. You nearly missed this plane."

"Ja, ja," he muttered and sat back to catch his breath.

A moment later the air vents began to murmur. Then came the whining of each engine as the huge jets stirred to life.

The airplane taxied to the end of a long runway, faced about, then flashed along the ground.

"We're in the air!" shouted Ricky, who was pressing his nose against the wide pane of glass.

As soon as the plane was high enough for seat belts to be unfastened, Pam and Holly took turns looking out of the window at the ocean sparkling far below.

Then the pigtailed girl kneeled on her seat and looked over the back of it. The stout man, who was wearing a jacket and vest, glanced up at her, scowling, then returned his eyes to the magazine he was reading.

Meanwhile Ricky wriggled out of his seat, crossed the aisle and pressed close to his brother.

"Who's that fellow sitting beside you, Pete?" he asked.

"I don't know yet," came the whispered reply. "Give me a little time."

Pete turned to address the passenger next to him. He had wavy, flaxen hair and deep-blue eyes. "I'm Pete Hollister, and our whole family is going to Germany," he said.

The boy, who was about fifteen, smiled. "My

name is Cliff Jager," he replied, "and I'm alone—on the way to visit my grandparents."

"Where do they live?" Pete asked.

"In Hornberg, in the Black Forest."

"Anywhere near Triberg, where we're going?"

"Just a few miles north of there," answered Cliff. "We'll be neighbors. That must be a valuable package," he added, eyeing the clock carton, which was on Pete's lap.

"Why do you say that?" the Hollister boy asked, surprised.

"Because you've been holding onto it so tightly," replied Cliff with a smile. "Why don't you put it in the overhead rack? Is it fragile?"

"I guess it could go there," Pete said. "It's a cuckoo clock."

Cliff's eyes twinkled. "Then it's going the wrong way. Most cuckoo clocks come out of Germany, not into it."

"This is a very special one," Pete said politely, but explained no more.

Although Cliff looked curious, he did not ask any further questions. Being taller than Pete, he helped the younger boy stow the package overhead.

Even before the plane had climbed to the altitude prescribed for the Atlantic crossing, Cliff Jager had been introduced to all of the Hollisters. The children liked the jolly boy at once and moved so that they could talk together better. Ricky and Holly perched

43

on the arms of the aisle seats and Pam sat in Holly's place with Sue on her lap.

When the youngsters learned from their new friend that he spoke German, they decided to take him into their confidence. Quietly Pete told him about the mystery of the cuckoo clock.

"Maybe I can help you when we get there," Cliff offered. He said that he liked to read detective stories but had never solved a real mystery himself.

Holly was getting restless. "Do you know any stories?" she asked.

"I know some legends about Germany," Cliff replied.

"Please tell us one," Pam begged.

Sue piped up loudly. "We'd 'preciate it." Everyone around chuckled except the stout man in the seat behind Holly's. He glowered and seemed to sink deeper into his chair, so that the lobes of his ears nearly rested on the top of his shirt collar.

"He reminds me of a turtle," Holly whispered.

"Shh," Pam warned the pigtailed girl. "He might hear you."

Cliff said his story was about a castle in Hornberg. He changed seats with Pete so that all could hear him.

"Once there was a baron who had a beautiful daughter," he began.

"Like Pam!" Sue whispered.

"Be quiet," Pam replied, blushing.

"Seeking for a suitable husband," Cliff went on,

"the baron picked a prince of the pagan Huns, but his daughter, although she fell in love with the prince, did not want to marry him because she was a Christian. So she fled from the castle, accompanied only by a pet doe, and lived in a cave."

"Did she take her coat with her?" Sue broke in.

"Yes," Cliff said, smiling, and continued with his story. "The beautiful girl wrote a prayer that the prince, too, might become a Christian. Then she died and the funeral was conducted by the baby deer."

"Oh goodness," Holly said, "isn't that sad!"

"Is that the end?" Ricky asked hopefully.

"No," Cliff went on. "There's more. Later, the prince became a Christian. One day he went out hunting in the nearby woods and suddenly was startled by a doe of remarkable beauty. He shot an arrow at it but missed, and the deer—"

"It was the same one, I'll bet!" Pam put in.

"Exactly." Cliff smiled. "This doe took him to the grave of the beautiful girl. There he read her prayer and decided to become a hermit."

"How sad can the story get!" Pete exclaimed.

"Oh, it's better near the end," Cliff said with a wink. "Then," he continued, "an angel disguised as a pilgrim visited the hermit. After partaking of his hospitality, the angel carried him to heaven where the beautiful girl lived."

Mr. and Mrs. Hollister had been listening to the

story also. They turned to praise Cliff on the way he had told it.

"Does the castle still stand today?" Mrs. Hollister asked.

"Yes, ma'am," the boy said, "and maybe you can all see it." Then he added, "Do any of you speak German?"

When they replied no, Cliff said, "Since you're working on a cuckoo clock mystery, how would you like to learn a song about a cuckoo?" He recited the words as the youngsters listened eagerly:

> *"Cuckoo, Cuckoo, ruf's aus dem Wald!*
> *Lassen uns singen, tanzen und springen,*
> *Cuckoo, Cuckoo, ruf's aus dem Wald!"*

Other passengers sitting nearby smiled when they heard this, and one woman who had a lovely soprano voice began to sing the song.

Before long, singing filled the airplane, amid laughter and handclaps.

"Yikes! Germany is going to be fun!" Ricky called out. Then he added, scratching his red hair, "What does the song mean?"

More laughter sounded through the airplane and a young man seated in front of Pete stood up in the aisle and, with gestures, recited:

> "Cuckoo, Cuckoo, calls us from the forest.
> Let us sing and dance and spring about.
> Cuckoo, Cuckoo, calls us from the forest."

46

"Oh, look at the funny bug on the ceiling," Ricky said.

Just then a stewardess walked down the aisle and said, "The singing is wonderful, but now it's time for dinner. Are you all hungry?"

Everyone chorused yes. The children went back to the seats and the stewardess put small pillows on their laps.

Moving quickly, the smiling young woman placed trays of delicious food on the cushions.

"Yummy!" Pam said. "I love pot roast."

"And mashed potatoes and peas and salad and popovers," Holly chimed in. "Oh, what's this in the little tube? Tooth paste?"

"Of course not, silly," Pam replied. "Don't you see? It says mustard."

Holly unscrewed the tiny cap and squeezed some light brown mustard on her meat. Ricky did the same, quietly watching Holly out of the corner of his eyes. Then he said, "Oh, look at the funny bug on the ceiling."

Taken by surprise, Holly looked up. But before she realized that her brother was joking, Ricky squeezed the mustard tube near her nose.

Squish!

A big blob ran the length of Holly's turned-up nose like Indian war paint. "Oh!" she exclaimed, and jerked away, accidentally pushing the button beside her seat. It tilted back and a loud voice boomed, "*Ach!* Look out, you're spilling my coffee!"

CHAPTER 6

A Word Game

QUICKLY Holly gave her tray to Pam and leaned over the back of the seat.

"Please excuse me," she said earnestly to the angry man. "I didn't mean to—"

"Look out!" the stout passenger roared. "You are dripping on me!"

Holly stared in dismay at the brown blob of mustard that had just dropped off her nose onto the man's knee.

"Oh," said the pigtailed girl, "I'm sorry."

The stout passenger's bristling gray hair seemed to stand even straighter and his red face now clearly showed a scar on his left cheek.

"All right, all right, don't do it again," the man said as Pam stood up to help her sister readjust the seat.

When it was fixed, Holly sat down and wiped the rest of the mustard off her nose.

"Yikes," Ricky said, grinning, "I'm sorry I caused so much excitement."

As soon as the two girls were settled with their trays again, Pam bent close to her sister's ear. "I saw something in that man's vest pocket. It looked like a little piece of wood."

When Holly stared blankly, Pam went on, "Don't you get it? That might be the cuckoo clock door."

"Oh!" Holly exclaimed, and clapped a hand over her mouth so as not to make too much noise. "Let's tell Daddy."

"I'll wait until we've finished eating," Pam said. "The man may suspect something if I go right away."

"What are you whispering about?" Ricky asked. His older sister told him softly.

Pam was so excited that she could hardly finish eating her dessert. Finally, however, the stewardess removed the trays. Pam slid out past Holly. She beckoned to Pete. When he followed, Pam wriggled in beside her father and told of her suspicion.

"How much of the cuckoo clock door did you see?" Mr. Hollister asked.

"Just the edge of it, Daddy. It was brown. I'm sure it was the door."

"We should not jump to conclusions," her mother cautioned. "It would be very embarrassing if we made a false charge against the man."

"Can't we have him arrested?" Pam asked.

Her father said he thought not, until they had proof of his guilt.

"I'll find the evidence," Pete declared. The boy told them he would walk up and down the aisle close to the passenger to get a better look at what was in his pocket. "And if it is the cuckoo clock door," Pete said stoutly, "we'll have our airplane captain arrest him."

With hands in his pockets, Pete sauntered up and down the aisle, each time glancing at the man behind Holly.

"I don't see anything in his vest pocket," Pete whispered to Pam after he had scrutinized the fellow twice.

"Oh, I'm sure I saw it," his sister replied.

"Okay, I'll take another look," Pete said.

Whistling the cuckoo clock tune, he strolled casually past the fat man again. But as he did, the plane suddenly lurched. Pete flung his hands out for support, but too late. He landed directly in the man's lap.

"Ooff!" the passenger cried out as the boy's weight nearly knocked the wind out of him. Spluttering in German, the man pushed Pete back into the aisle. Before the boy had a chance to apologize, the man blurted out *Dummkopf!* and waddled to the back of the plane to take a vacant seat.

Pete's face was still red with embarrassment as he sat down beside Cliff. "What did he say to me?" Pete asked his new friend.

Cliff chuckled and replied, "First he called you a stupid ox and when he left he said *dummkopf*. That means dumbhead."

When Pete's heart stopped racing, the boy thought to himself, "Maybe we're not so smart after all. If

"Ooff!"

that man is perfectly innocent, we have been very rude to him."

Pam glanced over questioningly at her brother and Pete shook his head no. He had not seen the cuckoo clock door.

When the stewardess walked down the aisle again, Pete reached out to touch her arm.

"Do you want another glass of milk?" the young woman asked with a smile.

"No, thank you," the boy said, "but could you tell me the name of that man who changed his seat?"

The stewardess walked to her station in the middle of the plane and returned shortly with a list of the passengers. "His name is Mr. Wetter," she said, "and he is going to Frankfurt."

"Thank you," Pete said, and asked Holly to change places with him.

He and Pam talked for several minutes about the mystery. "We could be wrong about Mr. Wetter," Pete remarked, but Pam was certain that she had seen the door.

"All right," Pete said, "suppose the man does have the cuckoo clock door. He would have split it open by this time and found that the note was missing."

"Of course," Pam agreed. "He probably did that right away. Then he must have guessed we had taken it out and rushed to follow us."

"He was late getting on the plane," Pete recalled.

"Another thing," his sister said, "he is German. And he did take the seat behind us."

"Pam, you must be right," said the boy. "This fellow is following us on account of the secret message. Do you still have it?"

"Yes—in my purse."

"*Psstt!*"

Pete turned his head to see what Holly was making the noise for.

The pigtailed girl motioned to the seat behind him and silently mouthed the words, "Mr. Wetter is back."

"Oh, maybe he heard us," Pam whispered.

The boy returned to his own place, worried about the turn of events. He looked thoughtfully out of the window. Below, fluffy moonlit clouds stretched as far as the eye could see, like the backs of a million woolly sheep.

It seemed certain to Pete that Mr. Wetter was mixed up in the mystery somehow, but there was no way they could prove anything, or hold the fellow for questioning.

"Say, Pete, what do you look so glum about?" Cliff Jager spoke up brightly.

"I was just thinking."

"Well, how about playing a game instead? Would you like to learn some more German?"

"By playing a game?"

"Sure, it's easy."

Pete beckoned to his brother and sisters, and the

children stood in the middle of the aisle as Cliff explained his game.

"Rhymes are the best way to learn words," Cliff said, and went on. "*Ja ist* yes. *Nein ist* no. *Ich weiss nicht ist* I don't know."

The Hollisters repeated slowly after him, and even some of the surrounding passengers took up the merry chant. Cliff continued: "*Kopf ist* head. *Katze ist* cat. *Rot ist* red. *Hut ist* hat."

"Hoot, hoot, hoot," Ricky said, rolling his eyes and making a silly face.

"Come on, be serious," Pam chided him. "We're learning a new language!"

After the children had repeated the rhymes several times, Cliff pointed to Ricky and asked, "*Ist der Kopf rot?*"

Holly giggled and said, "*Ja!*"

Then he pointed directly to her and asked, "*Ist der Hut am Kopf?*" The other children replied, "*Nein!*"

Cliff turned to Pam. "*Ist die Katze schwarz?*"

"*Ja, und nein,*" Pam said. "Our cat is black but has a white nose."

By the time they had finished playing their word game, the cabin lights went out. The stewardess provided blankets and pillows for the children and soon they were asleep.

To Pete it seemed he had only dozed off, when the lights went on again and the cabin stirred with activity. Soon breakfast trays were being passed about, and a thin, white line of light glowed on the northern horizon.

"That was a short night," Pete remarked to Cliff.

"I'll say. It lasted only two hours." The older boy explained that on flights eastward across the ocean, travelers lost five hours. "When we land in Germany," he said, "it will be seven o'clock there, but only two o'clock in New York."

Pete grinned. "Where do the hours go?"

"Oh, you'll get them back again on the return trip," Cliff told him.

After breakfast, the pilot announced that they were an hour from Frankfurt. "The weather is overcast and we should land in the rain," he informed them.

"But look how bright the sun is up here," said Sue as she shielded her eyes from the golden glare.

Now the airplane started the long descent. It dropped into a layer of black clouds, and raindrops splashed across the windows. Finally the children felt a gentle bump as the big craft touched down lightly on the runway.

"Hurray, we're in Germany!" Ricky cried out.

"*Ja, ja,*" Holly said.

As the family left the airplane, Mr. Wetter was close behind.

"I don't like the idea of his following us," Ricky told Pam softly. "He gives me the creeps."

After showing the customs man their passports, the Hollisters went to collect their baggage. Mr.

Wetter was not among the passengers claiming luggage. "If he didn't have any," Pete thought, "it's another sign that he rushed onto that plane just to trail us."

The family took a limousine from the airport into the city of Frankfurt. The rain beat down on top of the car in a lively tattoo, at the same time obscuring the view of the countryside.

"Maybe we were wrong about Mr. Wetter," Holly commented. "We might never see him again."

The two older children did not speak, but both of them thought the stout man would follow them.

After driving past open fields, the car went through the outskirts of town, finally coming into the center of the city and stopping in front of a new hotel.

A doorman carrying an umbrella ushered them inside of the building. The lobby was beautifully decorated in the latest mode, and as Mr. Hollister signed for his family at the desk, the children glanced about them in awe.

"Everybody is talking German," Ricky said as he stared at the people bustling to and fro.

Holly had wandered toward the front door where she stopped suddenly and raced back to Pam.

"He's here, he's here!" she cried out.

"Where did you see him?"

"I didn't," Holly said, "but a man standing next to the door called out, '*Ach Donnerwetter!*' That's his name!"

CHAPTER 7

A Redheaded Elf

WHEN the clerk overheard Holly's excited report, he leaned over the counter and smiled. "*Donner-wetter*," he repeated. "Yes, it is that. We have had rain here for two days." Then, seeing the bewildered look on the children's faces, he explained that *Donnerwetter* meant bad weather.

"*Donner* is a German word for thunder," he said, "and *Wetter*, of course, means weather. It is also an exclamation," he said.

"Like 'yikes!'?" Ricky asked.

"Something like it," the clerk replied.

"I'm going to call that fat man *Donnerwetter*," Holly spoke up.

By now the porter had beckoned to the family to follow him on the elevator. The visitors were led to their rooms on the third floor of the hotel. Their quarters were not connected, but were side by side at the end of a long corridor. Mr. and Mrs. Hollister went into one room, Pam, Holly and Sue the next, while Pete and Ricky walked into the third. Two single beds occupied one wall of the boys' room. Ricky promptly bounced on the nearest one and claimed it for his, while Pete began to unpack his bag.

In the girls' room there was a double bed and a cot for Sue. Holly peeked into the bathroom and exclaimed, "Oh, look! The bathtub is almost as large as a swimming pool!"

Pam and Sue joined the pigtailed girl in exploring the foreign-type bathroom. The tub was deep and long.

"I can float in it," Sue said happily.

"And look at the waterspout. It comes out of the wall!" Pam declared.

Holly was first to notice a button within easy reach of the bathtub. "What's this for, Pam?" she asked.

Her older sister did not know and Holly said, "Let's push it and find out."

"Oh, don't do that," Pam replied, "we don't know what might happen."

"Maybe we'll all go down the drain," Sue declared and shook her black bobbed hair.

"I'm so sleepy," Holly said, stretching her arms and yawning. "I think I'll take a bath and then go to bed."

Pam thought this was a good idea because really it was still the middle of the night in the United States.

The girls were roused from their slumber by a light tapping on the door. Pam jumped up, opened it and let her mother in.

"It's nearly noon," Mrs. Hollister said. "Time for you sleepyheads to have some lunch."

After the girls had dressed and combed their hair, they met Pete, Ricky and their parents in the hallway and stepped onto the elevator. But instead of going down, they went up.

"The restaurant is on the roof," their father said. "From there we will have a good view of the city."

When the elevator stopped at the roof garden the visitors were ushered to a table on the terrace overlooking the city below. The rain had ceased and the sun peeked occasionally through the cloudy sky.

The waiter handed each of the family a large white menu card upon which the names of the food were written both in English and German.

"Ha, here's a word I know—knockwurst!" Pete said. "I want some of that."

After Pam had ordered a beef sandwich, she glanced about her at the other tables. "Look!" she said. "There's a man who resembles Donnerwetter!"

"Where?" Pete asked.

"Over there, on the other side of the terrace." The diner, who had his back turned to them, was a stout man with bristly gray hair.

"We can't be sure he's the same man," their father said, pointing out that many German men were short, stout and had bristly gray hair.

"But may I look and see, Dad?" Pete asked.

Mr. Hollister nodded and cautioned his son to do so quietly. "And if it is, don't land in his lap again."

Pete pushed back his chair, and took a round-about route through the tables. As he was halfway to the man, the diner rose from his chair and began to walk from the room. Pete followed him and soon they were both out of sight in the restaurant foyer.

Pam was worried. "Oh dear, I hope Pete is all right."

"Maybe I'd better take a look-see," her father said, and hurried off after his son. Much to his surprise, he found Pete chatting amiably with the man near the elevators.

"Dad, I'd like you to meet Mr. Nebel," Pete said.

The man, who had light blue eyes, smiled with a humorous expression. "I'm not Mr. Donnerwetter, as you can see," he said with a German accent.

"I hope you'll pardon us," Mr. Hollister went on. "A case of mistaken identity. You say your name is Nebel? I have to see a man by that name at the World Toy Company today."

"Are you Mr. Hollister from the States?" the German asked in surprise.

"Don't tell me you're Mr. Nebel the toy manufacturer," Mr. Hollister said, raising his eyebrows.

"None other," the man declared, enjoying the joke and shaking hands with Pete and his father.

Mr. Hollister explained to his son that he and the company owner had corresponded and arranged an appointment at the display room of the factory that afternoon.

"Well, you found the right man after all," Mr. Nebel told Pete as he stepped onto the elevator. "I'll look forward to seeing you later."

When father and son returned to their table, the rest of the family were intrigued by the story of Pete's discovery.

"Small world," Mrs. Hollister said with a happy sigh.

"Yikes!" Ricky said. "The good guys and the bad guys sometimes look alike."

"From the back," Pam quipped, as she cut a piece of delicious German cake with her fork.

After finishing lunch, the Hollisters returned to their rooms before leaving on the trip to the toy factory.

"Come on, Sue, it's time to go," Holly called and Pam added, "Sue, where are you?" They glanced into the bathroom where the little girl was standing on a stool about to press the button on the wall.

"Don't do that!" Pam said. "Come, Mother and Daddy are waiting for us."

The family left the hotel entrance to find a large black automobile at the curb.

"Crickets, a Mercedes-Benz!" Pete declared.

"I rented it for our trip," their father said, and Pete secretly wished he were old enough to drive. Before setting off, Mr. Hollister consulted a road map of Frankfurt, then proceeded to the toy factory on the outskirts of the large city.

"Here we are," he said finally, pulling up in front of a large, modern building. The big glass windows on the first floor were filled with toys and colorful displays.

Inside the door they were greeted by Mr. Nebel. He bowed and shook hands as he was introduced to Mrs. Hollister and the rest of the children.

"First I will show you displays for your store window," the German said. "Come this way." He led them into a large room filled with the most wonderful figures the children had ever seen.

"It's like *Alice in Wonderland* and a Thanksgiving Day parade all put together," Pam remarked as she looked about. One group showed Santa Claus riding in a rocket which was pulled by eight reindeer.

"Look at this!" Holly pointed to Hansel and Gretel in a gingerbread house.

Mr. Nebel said, "Pull hard on the door handle." Holly did and it came right off in her hand!

"Oh!" she exclaimed.

"Taste it," Mr. Nebel said, grinning. When the pigtailed girl nibbled a little piece, she looked up, amazed. "This is candy!" She offered the handle to the other children and each broke off a part.

The toyman said that only the handle was made to be eaten, and he had a whole supply of them.

"Could we have the gingerbread house for our store, Daddy?" Sue pleaded.

"Here's one I like better," Pam said. She walked over to a group of elves and gnomes who formed a little orchestra.

The toymaker told them that this was one of his latest designs. The figures were Santa Claus's helpers having a party after the holidays were over. Mr. Nebel placed his finger on the tip of a dwarf's long nose and pressed a button there.

Instantly all the little figures began to move. The violinist played. Tiny cheeks puffed out as horns tootled and one little elf banged on the top of a toadstool with his drumstick.

"Imagine that in our Trading Post window at Christmas time!" Pete cried delightedly.

Mr. Hollister consulted with Mr. Nebel, and agreed to purchase the elf orchestra.

"We can have it shipped to America in time for Christmas," the toyman promised. Then he went on, "Our dolls are manufactured upstairs. Would you care to see how it's done?"

"Oh yes!" the three girls chorused. The Hollisters and their guide took an elevator to the next floor and entered a vast room where scores of women sat at sewing machines. In front of them on racks was an odd assortment of arms, legs, bodies, heads and wigs.

Mr. Nebel explained that the various parts of the dolls were made separately. "Each woman sews and stuffs a different item," he explained as he led them through the busy factory. The workers smiled up at

"Imagine that in our Trading Post window!"

the children as they passed. Pam lingered to watch doll dresses being skillfully decorated with ruffles and bows.

Then Mr. Nebel called to her, "Here is where the faces are painted." He showed them into a small room where half a dozen men and women sat at a long bench. Each had a doll's head in his hand and was busy painting eyes, nose, mouth and dimples.

"Oh, they're the sweetest things!" Holly declared.

Mr. Nebel stopped beside a pretty, blonde-haired woman and spoke to her in German.

"*Jawohl*," she said and glanced up into Pam's face. After studying it a moment, her fingers moved the paint brush deftly and she made the doll's face look just like Pam's!

"When this is finished, I will send it to you," she said, and added, "The pretty little girls will have their own dolls, too." Sue dimpled and Holly smiled impishly while the woman artist painted faces to look just like them.

"We have a redheaded boy doll, too," Mr. Nebel said.

Ricky looked embarrassed. "Not me! I'm not going to have a doll face!"

"Oh, please," his mother said.

"*Kommen Sie hier.*" The artist beckoned the red-haired boy.

Ricky looked about for escape and his eyes fell

upon the door. He raced over, opened it and vanished.

"Come back, Ricky!" Pam called after him, but the boy was gone.

Pete grinned. "I wouldn't like to have a doll face either," he said.

The children and their parents thanked Mr. Nebel for the tour of the toy factory.

"We have fire engines and space suits and toy animals, too," the owner said. "They are made in another factory. Perhaps sometime you would like to see them."

Mr. Hollister accepted the offer, and added, "My children have a mystery to solve in the Black Forest. When we return, we will visit you again, Mr. Nebel."

They went downstairs and out of the building, but Ricky was not at the car.

"Goodness, where did he go?" Mrs. Hollister asked.

"Ricky, Ricky!" Pam called and Pete glanced up and down the street. No Ricky.

"Do you suppose he's still in the factory?" Holly asked.

They all went inside and looked around the big display room. The elves were still playing a merry tune. Pam glanced at them and smiled, then jerked her head about quickly for a second look. She clapped her hand over her mouth to suppress a wild giggle. Standing beside the elf who was drumming on the toadstool was her brother Ricky. He moved his head up and down mechanically, and with his right hand beat on the toadstool like the elf beside him.

"There's Ricky!" she cried out. "Look, he's one of the elves!"

"What're you doing?" Pete asked.

The red-haired boy grimaced, and walked sheepishly toward his parents.

"Playing with the elves," he said. "I didn't want to be a doll."

"Oh, come, come," Mrs. Hollister said, putting an arm around him. "Nobody said that you *had* to be one."

On the way back to the hotel, Mr. Hollister drove his family around the city to look at interesting old buildings, fountains and the brand-new center of town.

After supper, when they went upstairs, Mr. Hollister gave Pete and Pam the keys to their rooms.

"Where are we going tomorrow, Daddy?" Pam asked.

"To Heidelberg, and next day the Black Forest."

"We'll work on the cuckoo clock mystery there," Pete said eagerly.

"Yes, and hunt a wooden lion for Mr. Spencer," his father added.

"Ugh!" said Holly, "I hope we don't see that awful Mr. Donnerwetter again."

"I think we're rid of him," her mother replied.

She kissed her daughters good night, and when Pam closed the door of the room behind her, she locked it.

For the next half hour, the three girls took turns splashing and rolling about in the huge tub. Holly was last. As she toweled herself dry, she looked up longingly at the button on the wall.

"Maybe elves will start playing a tune if I push it," she thought. Her small hand reached up gingerly and a finger pressed firmly against the button.

Holly waited but nothing happened. Then she slipped into her pajamas and was about to leap into her bed when suddenly there was a light knock on the door as the handle turned.

Before Pam had a chance to answer it, a key grated in the lock and the door opened slowly.

CHAPTER 8

The Old Ruins

"WHO is it?" Pam cried out in alarm as the door opened wider. A maid, wearing a black dress and white cap, peered inside. She asked a question in German that Pam could not understand.

Then, smiling, the woman walked to the bathroom and pointed to the push button.

"Oh, was that for calling the maid?" Pam asked in surprise.

The woman nodded yes and with a heavy accent said, "Do you not speak German?"

"Yes, we speak German," Holly said without hesitation and repeated, "*Ja ist* yes, *Nein ist* no, *Ich weiss nicht ist* I don't know."

The maid began to chuckle and Sue went on:

"*Kopf ist* head, *Katze ist* cat, *Rot ist* red, *Hut ist* hat."

At this the servant held her sides and laughed loudly. The noise attracted the two boys in the next room. They tapped on the door and walked in to see Pam giggling so hard that tears were in her eyes. When she told them that Sue and Holly were practicing their German, Ricky said to the maid, "I can sing in German, too. Cuckoo, cuckoo, *ruf's aus dem Wald*."

This caused the maid to laugh so hard that she slumped down into a chair and wiped her eyes with her apron.

Just then, the children's parents stepped into the room and laughed, too, at the funny episode. The maid excused herself, still chuckling tearfully, and Pam warned her brothers, "Don't ever push that button unless you want the maid."

"Don't worry," said Ricky. "Dolls! Maids! Yikes!"

When Mrs. Hollister kissed her daughters good night again, she said, "I hope we have as much fun tomorrow at Heidelberg. I hear it's a delightful place with a big castle overlooking the Neckar River."

"That reminds me," Mr. Hollister said, "you children may want to buy souvenirs, so I'll give you some money." As he handed each child an allowance, they thanked him.

"Now then," Mrs. Hollister said, "off to sleep so you'll be fresh for our trip." In a few minutes lights were out.

Before departing early the next morning, the youngsters looked around the lobby and in front of the hotel, but there was no sign of the suspicious Mr. Wetter.

While they were scouting, Ricky spotted a perky red cap in a little shop. "Yikes," he thought, "I

71

could buy that. I have money and I know how to say red hat."

He entered the store and said to the woman clerk, "*Rot Hut.*" With a smile she got the hat. Ricky paid for it and hurried back to the others, proudly wearing his purchase.

Everyone admired the cap. "Oh," said Holly, "it's just yummy. I'd like to wear it for a while. May I, Ricky?"

"Not now. When we reach Heidelberg, I'll let you try it," he promised.

Lightheartedly, the family climbed into the big black automobile and set out on their trip. It did not take long for their father to reach the Autobahn, a broad, straight, four-land highway.

As the children watched the countryside roll by, Holly's eyes strayed now and then to the red cap on Ricky's head. How she would like to wear it! But Holly only sighed and tried to be patient.

After traveling several hours they came to the outskirts of Heidelberg. "I see the river!" Ricky called out.

"That must be the Neckar," Pam said.

The road led along the river and in the distance they could see an ancient stone bridge.

"That's called the *Alte Brücke,*" Mrs. Hollister said, consulting the guidebook. On the far side "the old bridge" was flanked by two stone towers, beyond which the town seemed to rise steeply against a mountain slope.

"Oh look!" Pete cried. "There's the castle!"

Part way up the hill was the huge ruin. Great walls and battlements towered high above the river. Holly and Pam were wide-eyed with excitement. It was the first real castle they had ever seen.

The instant Mr. Hollister drove onto the narrow stone bridge, Holly reached over and lifted the red cap from Ricky's head.

"Now it's my turn," she declared.

"When the car stops you can have it," Ricky said.

"But we're already in Heidelberg!" Holly held the hat behind her. Ricky jerked it away so hard that the cap flew out the window over the narrow bridge and into the river!

"Yikes, my hat!" Ricky exclaimed. "Please, Daddy, stop the car!"

"It's no use, Ricky," Mr. Hollister replied. "It's gone."

Ricky bit his lip to keep back tears.

"I'm sorry," said Holly in a small voice. "I'll buy you a new one with my money."

Mr. Hollister drove between the two towers at the end of the bridge, turned right and parked in front of an old hotel.

While their father went inside with Mrs. Hollister and Sue to see about rooms, the other children skipped across the street to watch the boats from the promenade on the riverbank.

Suddenly Ricky seized Pete's arm. "Look!" he

73

cried, pointing to a rowboat in the middle of the river. "There's my hat!"

In the skiff were three youths, one of them wearing a red hat. The other two had blue caps with crimson and white stripes.

"There's an empty rowboat," Pete said, pointing down the bank a little distance. "We'll borrow it." The children ran to the skiff, and while the girls waited, Pete and Ricky quickly rowed out toward the three young men.

"Ahoy!" the redhead called to catch their attention. "*Hut—hut!*" He pointed to the hat and to his own head.

The trio in the boat laughed and pulled near to the boys. The tallest one wore the red cap perched high on his curly blond head.

When the two boats were side by side, Ricky tried to show by gestures how his cap had flown off the bridge.

"*Ja, ja, ja!*" The big youth chuckled. "I like your hat," he said in careful English. "It fits me so well." His companions laughed heartily and the two boys grinned.

"We are students at Heidelberg University," the fellow went on. "Would you like one of our hats for a souvenir?"

"Yikes," Ricky said, "that would be keen."

"Good. We trade."

The blond youth took a striped cap from his pocket and offered it to Ricky. The boy stood up

74

Ricky hung like a bridge.

and reached for it. Just then a large oil tanker chugged past and huge swells nearly swamped the rowboats.

With a cry Ricky teetered and fell toward the other boat, and his fingers clutched the gunwale. He hung like a bridge and cried out for help as the waves slapped at his chest.

Quickly the students and Pete nudged the rocking boats together. Ricky was saved!

"That was your initiation into Heidelberg," said the blond youth, grinning. "Here's your student hat." He tossed it to Ricky, who thanked him, and Pete rowed back.

When the redhead hopped onto the promenade he proudly showed his new cap and wet front to prove his story. Then the children all ran to help Mr. Hollister carry the luggage into the hotel.

"Where is the elevator?" Pete asked the woman clerk.

She smiled and said there was none. They would have to carry their baggage up one flight of the old, dimly lit marble staircase.

"Yikes, this is spooky!" Ricky said, running his hand along the cool, stone rail as he ascended the stairs with the others.

The three rooms the family occupied had tall ceilings and old-fashioned marble washbasins.

"This is like living a hundred years ago," Pete told Ricky as they went downstairs again to join the others.

"Now we'll go to the castle," their father said.

They walked along a narrow street on a sidewalk hardly wide enough for two persons to pass. Pam held Sue by the hand for fear she might step off the curb into the path of the small automobiles that drove by.

The little street led into a large cobblestone square, surrounded by ancient buildings. The Hollisters picked their way carefully through the crowds of students and sight-seers as they walked on toward the castle, which now loomed high above them.

"Yikes, I didn't know it was so steep!" Ricky said. He scrambled ahead, up a trail flanked on the right by an immense stone wall.

Up and up they trudged. Mr. and Mrs. Hollister stopped for a moment to glance back on the town and river that now lay below them.

"Come on, Mommy, come on, Dad. Hurry," Holly called out. "We're knights storming the castle!"

"Huh," Ricky said, "whoever heard of a knight with pigtails."

"Come on, I'll race you," the tomboy challenged, and the two children ran up a long flight of stone steps. Reaching the top, they came to a vast courtyard bordered on the riverside by a steep parapet.

"Crickets! You can see for miles around!" Pete said when he and Pam caught up. Awed, the children looked behind them at the ruined castle.

"How beautiful it must have been in courtly days!" Pam remarked dreamily.

"I'll bet there were some fierce battles here," Pete commented.

"You're right," Mrs. Hollister said and told them that she had read the history of the castle the evening before. "In 1688 Louis XIV of France sent an army which conquered Heidelberg. A year later," she went on, "the French were forced to leave. But before they did, the troops set fire to the castle and blew up several towers."

Sue held her hands over her ears and winced.

"Don't worry. There won't be any more explosions," Pete assured her as their mother continued.

"The French came back in 1693, but this time," Mrs. Hollister said sadly, "the castle was reduced to a heap of ruin and the town was burned to ashes by the soldiers."

"I want to see where the explosion was," Ricky said.

They set off again over the cobblestone pavements, walking up through another courtyard into beautiful gardens surrounded by a low stone fence.

Sight-seers of all ages and nationalities strolled about admiring the old ruins. Finally, Pete and Pam spied a stone tower which seemed to have been cut in half, showing two gaping black rooms.

"Ricky, here's where the blowout must have been," Pete called.

A German passer-by smiled and nodded. *"Ja,"*

he said, "that is the famous blown-up tower. It was a place to store gunpowder."

Ricky's eyes opened wide when he saw it, and he wanted to climb into the old fortress, but he soon saw that there was no way of scaling the crumbling walls.

As the family gazed at the ruin, Sue tugged on Pam's hand and said, "I'm thirsty. I want a drink. I see a good place." She pointed across a broad walk to a little shop advertising refreshments.

"Here," Mr. Hollister said to Pete, and gave him a handful of German coins. "Bring mother and me a drink, too."

The children hastened over to a woman standing behind the counter.

"*Was willst du haben?*" she asked. Then, seeing them hesitate, she went on with a smile. "What will you have? How about some German *apfelsaft?*"

"What is that?" Pam asked.

The woman told them that it was sweet apple cider which came in small chilled bottles. While she snapped off the caps and inserted little straws in the drinks, a small, dark-haired man moved close to Pam's side. As she reached out for the *apfelsaft*, the stranger snatched her handbag and dashed away.

"Halt!" shouted the woman.

"Stop!" Pam cried out, as the man zigzagged through a crowd of tourists.

CHAPTER 9

A Shy Bird

PETE darted after the man, who headed in the direction of Mr. Hollister.

"Catch him, Dad!" Pete called out.

Several passers-by stood shoulder to shoulder with Mr. Hollister so as to trap the fugitive, but the little man, clutching Pam's handbag close to his chest, dived between Mr. Hollister's legs, rolled over several times and scrambled to his feet.

Pete dashed past the startled grownups and with a burst of speed gained on the purse snatcher. The pursued man made a sudden turn to the left and threw the pocketbook over an iron fence.

As the fugitive scampered down a long, stone ramp, Pete and the others hastened to the rail and looked down. The purse lay on the green grass of a sunken garden, thirty feet below, at the foot of the blown-out tower. A short, stocky man was walking quickly toward the handbag.

"It's Mr. Wetter!" Pete exclaimed.

At that moment a guard stepped through a low archway, spotted the purse nearby and picked it up just before the stout man could do so.

"That's our bag!" Ricky cried down. "Don't give it to him!"

"Arrest that man!" Pete shouted.

The guard looked up at the crowd gathering along the railing and cupped a hand to his ear.

"Oh, he doesn't understand us!" Mrs. Hollister said.

Recognizing the Hollisters, Mr. Wetter hurried off through the archway.

"Oh, catch him, catch him!" cried Pam and Holly.

Someone in the crowd shouted to the guard in German. The uniformed man nodded and motioned to the Hollisters that he would return the bag.

"Isn't that the limit!" Mrs. Hollister exclaimed. "If we could only make that attendant understand Mr. Wetter is the real thief!"

The Hollisters all agreed that the portly man probably had hired the pickpocket to grab Pam's handbag and drop it into the sunken garden, where he would be waiting to retrieve it.

"We might as well drink our *apfelsaft* while we're waiting," Mr. Hollister said, and the visitors returned to the refreshment stand. Just as they finished their delicious drinks, the guard approached them.

Pam thanked him when he returned the handbag to her. With the help of the woman who sold the drinks, the Hollisters made him understand that

Wetter had been shadowing the family ever since they had left America.

The guard apologized for not catching the man, but said that he would report the incident to the police.

"Oh, that mean Mr. Donnerwetter!" Holly said, stamping her foot. "We almost had him!"

As they made their way back to the hotel, Mrs. Hollister told the others that she felt uneasy. "The secret of the cuckoo clock must be an important one," she said, "for Mr. Wetter to try so hard to get hold of that note."

Pete agreed. "I think the real clues to the mystery are in Triberg," he added. "The sooner we get there, the better."

"We are starting for the Black Forest first thing in the morning," Mr. Hollister advised them.

"Good," said Pam as they walked into the old hotel. "But we will have to keep our eyes open for Mr. Wetter. He'll probably try again to get the note."

Before they set out next day, Pam opened her purse in the hotel lobby and gave Pete the mysterious message. "You keep it," she said. "Nobody's going to steal your handbag."

Her brother tucked the tiny paper inside his wallet, returned it to his hip pocket and buttoned down the flap.

Then they hurried out, got into the car and started along the Autobahn toward Triberg. After a few miles, deep-green, pine-clad hills appeared on the left side of the highway.

"There's the beginning of the Black Forest," Mr. Hollister announced.

"I think I know why they call it that," Pete said. "The dark-green trees look almost black from a distance."

Holly gave a delicious shudder and declared that the woods must be full of gnomes and gingerbread witches.

"And cuckoo birds too," Sue added. "I'd like to catch one."

"To put in a clock?" Ricky teased her.

"Yes, and I'd feed it some bread crumbs every time it cuckooed."

The broad highway now was marked every mile or so by rest areas at the side of the road. After nearly an hour's ride, Mr. Hollister drove into one and parked his car near several smaller European automobiles. The doors of the Hollister car flew open and the children scampered out to breathe deeply of the sweet woodland air.

"Oh, look! There's an American car!" Pam said, pointing to an auto a few yards ahead of them.

"It has an Illinois sticker on the window," Pete remarked as he and Pam approached. Seated on campstools beside the car were a young man, a woman and a girl about Pam's age.

"Hello," Pete said. "Are you Americans?"

"Are we!" the girl exclaimed delightedly. "Oh,

it's so good to hear someone from home!" The girl introduced herself as Gladys Renner. She had short, curly brown hair and merry blue eyes.

"We live in Germany because Daddy works here," she said. "Now we are taking a holiday and driving to Switzerland."

As they talked together, Sue approached shyly with Ricky and Holly running along behind her.

"We're looking for cuckoo birds," Sue declared.

"You came to the right place," Mr. Renner said and pointed to the woods. "There are some here but they are very shy. If you are lucky you may hear one, but they keep out of sight."

"If you do hear a cuckoo," Gladys said, "and have a coin in your pocket at the time, it's supposed to bring you good luck."

"We could use some good luck," Pete remarked, and Pam knew he was thinking of the mystery.

Just then Mr. Hollister called, "Oh, Pete, lend me a hand, will you? We have a soft tire here and I think we'd better change it."

Pete ran back to the Mercedes-Benz, with Ricky at his side.

"Okay, Dad," the red-haired boy said. "We'll both help!"

Mrs. Hollister, who had been looking at a road map, stepped out of the car and continued studying their route while the three Hollister menfolk went to work changing the wheel.

When the fresh tire was securely in place, Ricky

glanced back toward the girls. They were not standing beside the Illinois car nor where they to be seen anywhere. Ricky scampered up to Mr. Renner. "Where did the girls go?" he asked.

"Into the woods a little way," the man replied. "They're looking for a cuckoo bird. They'll be back in a minute or two."

Ricky was disappointed that he had not joined them. Thrusting his hands deep into his pockets, he sauntered back toward Pete, who was wiping his hands on an old cloth. The redhead reported what he had been told. "They're cuckoo if you ask me," he said, "trying to find a bird when we're in such a hurry."

Pam and Gladys, meanwhile, followed by Sue and Holly, walked along a recreation path leading into the woods. Now and then they stopped to listen. Silence.

"I don't hear anything," Holly said. "Maybe the birds cuckoo only on the hour."

Pam and Gladys giggled and Pam said, "Here's the end of the path and we haven't heard one."

"I think we'd better go back," Gladys remarked. *Cuckoo, cuckoo, cuckoo.*

"What's that?" Holly said, startled.

"You made that noise, Pam, didn't you?" asked Sue.

Their sister's face brightened and she said, "Girls, that was a cuckoo bird, I'm sure."

The four children stood still and listened. From

far off in the woods came the clear cry, *cuckoo*, *cuckoo*.

"That sounds just like our clocks," Holly said and her fist doubled over a German coin she had in her pocket. "Hurray, we're lucky!" Then she added to herself, "Now we'll solve the mystery for sure!"

The birdcall came again. This time it seemed closer.

"Oh, I wish we could see the cuckoo," Pam said.

"Then why don't we go look?" Holly demanded. "It must be nearby."

Pam glanced about her, making a mental note of the landscape. "All right," she said, "we'll go into the woods a little way, but not too far."

Holding hands, the four girls made their way through the towering pine trees, walking softly so as not to disturb the cuckoo. Their gaze was fixed high among the branches, but they did not see any birds at all.

"There, I hear it again!" Gladys exclaimed, but this time the call seemed farther away.

"Ho hum, it must be a shy bird like me," Holly said.

This made Pam grin and she replied, "Whoever heard of a shy tomboy, Holly?" She added, "We'd better turn back now. The sky is getting dark. It looks like rain."

"Oh please, let's go a little farther," Holly begged. "Daddy and Mother won't mind."

"All right," Pam said finally. "Another hundred steps and then we'll go back."

As they walked forward, the wind began to sigh through the topmost branches of the evergreens. But now the cuckoo bird was silent.

"Maybe it's gone back to its nest on account of the rain coming," Sue declared.

"Ninety-eight, ninety-nine, one hundred," Gladys counted off the steps. "Now let's go back," she said, a little frightened.

The four girls turned about and, as they retraced their steps, the wind began hissing through the trees. Dark clouds suddenly swept low over the woods, nearly touching the tops of the complaining firs.

"Yikes!" Holly said, imitating her brother, "we might find a gingerbread witch instead of a cuckoo bird if we don't hurry."

Sue and Holly broke into a run ahead of the older girls, and Pam quickly called them back. "Not that way. Over here," she said. "You're going in the wrong direction."

"This is the way we came," Holly replied. "I'm sure." But she obeyed her older sister and the girls trotted through the darkening forest.

When they had gone far enough to have returned to their starting place, Pam's heart began to beat wildly. She looked about her. There was no path, no road and no cars to be seen.

"Oh dear!" Pam whispered. *"We must be lost."*

Pam stood still and listened. Then she cried out, "Mother, Daddy!" No reply.

"Oh dear!" she whispered. "We must be lost."

"Goodness," Gladys said, "we're probably traveling in circles."

"Every direction looks the same," Holly said anxiously, glancing at the tall trees all around them.

Sue slipped her hand into Pam's and held tight. Now the wind whistled and wailed and ruffled their hair as the girls pressed on through the woods.

"I think we ought to stand still," Pam said finally, "so we won't get lost any worse than we are."

Cuckoo, cuckoo, cuckoo. The sounds came from a little glen off to their left.

"It's a bird!" Holly cried out.

Suddenly the air was filled with cuckoo calls.

"There must be a nest full of them!" Sue said, as a tiny drop of rain splashed against her cheek.

Pam and Gladys, too, were intrigued by the bird noises and set off in their direction.

The calls grew louder and louder as the four girls drew closer to a small ravine. Getting down on hands and knees, they peered over the edge. In the glen below them was a little tent, and in front of it stood two girls and a boy. Their hands were cupped to their faces and they called loudly, "Cuckoo, cuckoo! Cuckoo, cuckoo!"

"Some birds!" Holly said with a wry face.

The four girls slid down the little embankment and approached the three other children. The trio spoke out in German. Gladys talked to them for a few minutes in the same language.

"What are they doing here?" Pam asked her new friend.

Gladys explained that the children were camping with their parents, who had gone to town for more supplies. The cuckoo call was their signal.

"They are afraid their mother and father won't find them in the gathering storm," Gladys said.

"Tell them that we'll stay with them and nothing bad will happen," Pam spoke up.

Gladys introduced the Hollister girls to the German youngsters and they all crawled into the tent. Now the rising wind made the canvas sides snap like a cracking whip. All the older children swallowed hard and tried to grin at each other. Sue cuddled close to Pam.

"*Mutti, mutti,*" whimpered the smaller German girl, who was about five years old.

"Don't worry, your mother will find us," Pam told her.

"Sure," Holly said. "We're lucky because we heard a—"

Whoosh! A strong gust of wind blew against the tent and flattened it over the heads of the children!

CHAPTER 10

A Slippery Slide

THE muffled screams of the children were drowned out by the howling wind. Holly was the first to crawl to freedom. As she poked her head out from under the flat of the tent she heard more cuckoo calls. They seemed to come from close by. Holly stood up and made an opening for the others to crawl out.

When the German children heard the cuckoo sounds, they burst into loud birdcalls themselves and presently a man and woman appeared out of the gloom.

Seeing seven youngsters beside the fallen tent, the man exclaimed in English, "The Hollisters! Are you the lost children?"

"Yes, sir," Pam said.

"And me, too," Gladys added, as the German couple came closer.

"Are you hurt?" the woman asked.

"No, we were just frightened," Pam said. "How did you know we were lost?"

"Your parents are looking for you."

"Where are Mommy and Daddy?" Sue asked. The

children were surprised to hear that the cars were parked only a short distance away.

"I will lead you to them," the man said. "My wife can help our children fix the tent."

Within minutes, the girls were back in the parking area. Quickly the Hollisters said good-by to Gladys, and the German hastened to rejoin his family.

"We're sorry we got lost," Pam said. "It was all on account of the cuckoo bird."

"Hurry! Get into the car," her mother said, "before the storm breaks."

They piled into the black automobile and slammed the doors shut just as a deluge rattled on the roof. Mr. Hollister set off along the highway and the girls excitedly told of their adventure.

A deep gloom hung over the forest. Thunder began to roll and lightning brightened the slippery road with great white flashes.

"Watch for the turnoff to Triberg," Mr. Hollister told everybody.

"There it is now!" Pete exclaimed, pointing to a sign down the road.

Their father drove off the Autobahn and onto a small, winding road. The *swish-click* of the windshield wipers could not keep up with the water that poured across the window glass.

The car slowed up to cross a small bridge, and as Mr. Hollister drove down the other side, the auto splashed through a deep puddle of water. Unable to see the edge of the road, he diminished his speed. They were crawling along in the blackness when there was a sudden jarring as the two right wheels dropped off the edge of the road. Mr. Hollister turned sharply to his right to keep from upsetting.

Bump, bump, bump! They were stuck in a ditch!

For a few seconds no one spoke. Then Ricky said, "Yikes! Wait until we tell the kids back home about this!"

Pam could hear the water gurgling beneath the car. "If it rains much longer we'll all have to swim out of here," she said, trying not to sound frightened.

Mr. Hollister remarked that it could be worse. At least they were off the road and would not bump into another car.

To pass the time, the youngsters sang the German cuckoo song and when they had finished with that, Pam said, "Let's sing our old bird song!"

"Oh, let's!" agreed Holly. "Ricky and I'll begin!" Lustily the whole family sang a round they had known for a long time.

> "Kookaburra sits in the old gum tree.
> Merry, merry king of the bush is he.
> Laugh, kookaburra,
> Laugh, kookaburra,
> Gay your life must be!"

"Well, things *are* getting gayer," Mr. Hollister observed as the rain let up and the dark clouds began to drift away.

By the time normal daylight had returned, the rain had ceased, and the only noise was the gurgling of the water in the ditch.

"Crickets, look where we are!" Pete declared, rolling down the car window.

The ditch was at the edge of a broad field. In the middle of it stood a neat chalet-type cottage.

On the front steps a man was donning boots. He made his way down a lane through the field and approached the Hollisters' car. Pam called out, "Do you speak English?"

"*Bisschen*—a little," came the reply, as the man doffed his rain hat.

"We can't get out of the car," Mrs. Hollister called.

"I will help you," the man replied and hastened to a barn adjacent to his house.

The Hollisters watched, amazed, as two powerful oxen lumbered out of the barn. The man led them along the lane, and attached a stout chain from the animals' harness to the front of the car. Then, at his command, the great beasts lowered their heads and dug their hoofs into the soft ground.

The car moved. Inch by inch, up out of the ditch it came as the oxen puffed and snorted. "*Jawohl. Gut!*" the man said, as the Mercedes-Benz was pulled onto the road.

94

The family got out and thanked the kind man. "May we pay you for your services?" Mr. Hollister asked.

"*Nein*," he said emphatically. Then, looking up into the sky, he added, "*Ach*, a Black Forest storm is no welcome to visitors. Come into my house. You must have something to eat and drink before you travel on."

The Hollisters thanked the man, and slowly followed in their car while he led the oxen up the lane to the barn.

As they mounted the porch steps Pete whispered to Pam that the German must be a farmer. But the boy changed his mind upon entering the house. The vast living room of the chalet had a fireplace at one end and was comfortably furnished with a huge rough table and sturdy leather-covered chairs. All about were wood carvings of various shapes and sizes.

"My name is Heinrich Brunner," he told the Hollisters and they introduced themselves.

"You must be a *Schnitzelmeister*," Pam said as the man bade them sit down at the table.

"No, not really a master," their host replied. "I like to carve in my spare time, and farm when the weather is good. Here, try some of my homemade cheese." He cut slices of dark bread and passed a platter of light-colored cheese.

When everyone had taken some, he poured out tall glasses of cool milk.

"You are very kind to us," Mrs. Hollister said, "and we thank you."

"You are touring the *Schwarzwald?*" the man inquired.

Mr. Hollister told him about their trip and the carved lion they were seeking. "Could you make one for us?" he asked.

The man shook his head. "No. What you seek is a real *Schnitzelmeister,*" he said. "There is one in Triberg. His name is Karl Fritz."

The Hollisters looked amazed. "Karl Fritz, the cuckoo clock maker?" Pete asked.

"*Ja, ja.* That's indeed the man," their host replied. "He is the best in all Germany."

While the Hollisters ate their bread and cheese, the man told them that Karl Fritz had learned his craft in Eastern Germany. "He came to Triberg after the war," he added. "The *Schnitzelmeister* has taught hundreds of wood carvers all over Germany. And he has classes for children, too."

"Oh, I want to be a *Schnitzel* girl!" Holly declared.

"*Ja,* Karl Fritz will show you. He can make the lion, too."

The family was pleased to learn that Triberg was not far away.

"Perhaps we can make reservations from here," Mr. Hollister said, noticing a telephone in the corner of the room.

Heinrich Brunner said he would be glad to do

this for them. The Park Hotel, he added, was the best. Quickly he put in a call. When he hung up, he smiled and said, "Herr Mueller, the proprietor, will be waiting for you."

After they had finished eating, the Hollisters said thank you and good-by and returned to their car. The wood carver watched them from his porch.

"Oh, I wish we could do something for this nice man," Mrs. Hollister said.

"Yikes, I know what!" Ricky exclaimed. "I can give him my Heidelberg University hat."

"Bless your heart," his mother said. "I know how you prize it. But if you would like to, you may offer it to him."

Ricky clutched the hat and ran toward the German. "Here's a present for you, Herr Brunner," he said. "I shan't be going to the University for a while yet."

The wood carver looked at the cap, then burst into a broad smile. *"Danke, danke,"* he said. "You are generous. I shall keep the hat and remember you." He set the student cap on his head, and stood waving to the Hollisters until the car reached the end of the lane and they drove away.

The tires hissed against the still-wet pavement that led them higher into the Black Forest. The valleys became narrower and for a while the road skirted a swollen mountain stream which foamed and bubbled over rocks and boulders.

"Here's Triberg, Dad!" Ricky suddenly said.

The sign pointed to a right-hand turn and they proceeded up a street steeper than any they had encountered. At first there were only a few houses, but as they approached the center of town, the buildings stood shoulder to shoulder on both sides of the cobbled pavement. Finally the road opened onto a broad town square. It, too, was built on a slope.

"There's not a level place in town," Mr. Hollister remarked, as he stopped in front of a building with the sign, Park Hotel.

When the family entered, a short, dark-haired man with a friendly smile greeted them. "The Hollisters from the States, I presume," he said with a little bow.

"You are Mr. Mueller?" the children's father asked.

"Yes, at your service."

Mr. Hollister smiled and replied, "We had to swim uphill all the way, but here we are."

"Your rooms are on the third floor," the proprietor said. "I will have a boy help you up with the luggage."

The carpeted stairway led to a large landing on the second floor. The bellboy, who was loaded with suitcases, smiled and said, "This is the first floor."

"Yikes!" Ricky said, "then our rooms are really on the fourth floor?"

The youth nodded and led the way up two more flights of stairs. At the top was a broad hall. Pete's and Ricky's room was on one side, and across from them were their parents and the girls.

The two large, high beds in the boys' room were covered with thick eider-down quilts. Ricky bounced into the middle of one. "Yikes, is it soft!" he exclaimed and rolled out again. He joined Pete who was gazing out the window at the gabled roofs of the town below them.

"Look," Ricky said, "there is a fire escape here." The boys climbed out of the window, stood on the iron grating and surveyed the hotel gardens below.

In a few minutes they popped back inside their room and hurried to another window that looked onto the street in front of the hotel. Then they unpacked their suitcases. Presently there came a knock on the door.

"Are you boys ready?" Mr. Hollister asked.

"Okay, Dad," they replied.

The family trooped down the stairs, but Ricky and Holly lingered behind. Each looked at the other with the same thought in mind. *Wouldn't it be keen to slide down the banister?*

Ricky and Holly straddled the slippery wood.

Zip! down they scooted, but before reaching the post they hopped off. The next banister was even longer. Holly got on first. Down she zipped, but became panicky at her speed. She quickly threw one leg over the banister, fell off and landed *kerplop!* on the stairs. *Bounce, bounce, bounce,* down the steps she went!

Zip!

"Goodness, what happened!" Mrs. Hollister exclaimed, turning about.

Holly picked herself up and straightened her dress as the seat of Ricky's pants squealed to a stop beside her.

"Children!" their mother reproved. "You are guests here. Behave yourselves."

Ricky and Holly promised not to slide on the banisters again. When they reached the comfortable lobby, their father was talking with Mr. Mueller.

"You say you know Mr. Fritz?"

"Yes, he's a friend of mine," the hotel man replied, "but he's not home today. He'll be back on Friday, the day after tomorrow."

"We have to see him about something very important," Pete said.

"Oh, you'll find him all right. His shop is near here," Mr. Mueller told them and excused himself to speak with another guest.

Outside, Pete remarked, "Dad, this feels like being on the deck of a tilting ship."

His father chuckled in agreement and noted that all the passers-by were carrying canes to help them walk on the steep hills.

By the time the family had gone down one side of the street and halfway up the other, Mr. Hollister decided that they needed canes, too. They stepped into a little shop where they all picked out walking sticks.

While Mr. Hollister was paying for their purchases, Pete noticed Sue looking longingly at a small red ball with flowers painted on it. He paid for it and gave it to his sister.

"Oh, thank you!" the little girl said, delighted. She turned the ball over and over in her chubby hands, admiring the colorful blossoms on it.

The rest of the afternoon the family explored the shops, and the children bought souvenirs for Uncle Russ, Aunt Marge, their cousins and all their friends in Shoreham.

Loaded with small parcels, the Hollisters headed for the hotel.

"I'm hungry," Ricky announced. "I could eat an elephant."

"We'll have supper as soon as we get back," Mr. Hollister said.

"And then off to bed," their mother added. "You all have had quite a day. Tomorrow we can explore the town."

After a delicious meal in the hotel dining room, the Hollisters went to bed and pulled their down comforters over them. No sooner had Pete laid his head on the pillow than he was fast asleep. He was startled awake by a strange noise.

Ta—ta—ta—ta a trumpet sounded in the morning stillness; then came the roll of drums. Pete glanced at his wrist watch. "Six A.M.," he said, "and a band is playing? Ricky, wake up, something is going on!"

CHAPTER 11

An Amazing Cat

THE two boys ran to the window and looked out. In the street below stood a group of young people with baskets full of flower petals. The band could not be seen, but the music sounded stirring in the morning stillness.

Just then the door opened and the three girls peeked in.

"What's happening?" Pam asked.

"Come in and see," Pete replied. "What do you think they are doing?"

The sisters looked down from the casement windows. Sue clapped her hands at the sight below.

"Oh!" Pam said, "I can't believe it. Pete, they are making a carpet of flowers in the street."

"Let's go and watch them," Holly suggested.

The girls scampered back to their room to dress hurriedly. A few minutes later they met the boys in the hall and all trooped downstairs.

In the front of the hotel were groups of youngsters carrying baskets of flowers. Some children were on their knees, arranging designs of red, white, purple and blue blossoms against a background of green grass two feet wide.

One girl about sixteen looked up and smiled. In English she said, "Have you never seen *Fronleichnam* before?"

"No, what is that?"

The girl stood up and brushed a strand of black hair from her forehead with the back of her hand. She told the Hollisters that *Fronleichnam* was Corpus Christi day, one of the chief religious holidays in the Black Forest.

"We are making a carpet of flowers to the church," she said, "and a procession will march over it."

"Wait until I tell Mom and Dad!" Ricky exclaimed, and dashed toward the hotel steps, nearly bumping into two porters placing a statue of a saint on the landing. One of the waitresses put a garland at the foot of it.

"When you come back, bring our camera!" Pete called as Ricky hurried inside.

By the time Mr. and Mrs. Hollister appeared, more people had gathered in the street. The carpet of flowers stretched longer and longer, and the young folks chatted quietly as their deft fingers arranged the blossoms.

While the Hollisters watched, fascinated, Pete snapped one picture after another.

Mr. Mueller came out and smiled broadly. "Quite a surprise for you, isn't it?" he asked. The proprietor told them that the youth of Triberg had gathered bushels of blossoms the day before. "I know you will enjoy our ceremony," he said. "It begins soon."

The Hollisters hastened into the hotel for a quick breakfast. They had just finished eating when they heard a band strike up again.

The family hurried to the street to see musicians in blue uniforms marching along the flower-bedecked street. They were led by several clergymen, and were followed by children dressed in what Grandmother Hollister would have called "their Sunday best." The faces of the little youngsters were bright and rosy, but they marched quietly down the steep street. Next came a group of policemen. After them marched men dressed in old German costumes of pantaloons, green jackets and wide-brimmed hats.

"What a long parade!" Holly remarked.

"It looks as if everybody in town is marching today," Pete said.

Now came another band playing a stately hymn. These musicians were followed by nuns and women dressed in white, embroidered costumes.

As the procession moved over the carpet of flowers, the blooms were scattered about the street. When the last parader had passed, the Hollisters joined the crowd, which fell in behind the marchers. Down the street they went, turned a corner, then another, and proceeded up a hill toward the church. Its beautiful lines stood out sharp and clear in the bright morning sunlight.

With the other tourists, the Hollisters entered the

crowded church. When the services had ended, the family returned to their hotel for lunch. The dining room was filled with visitors who had come to Triberg for the occasion.

"What will we do until Mr. Fritz comes back?" Ricky asked impatiently.

"We'll see the town's main attractions," his father said. "They have a waterfall here that is the highest one in Germany."

"Like Niagara Falls, you mean?" asked Holly, spooning up a big glob of strawberry ice cream with whipped cream on top.

"We'll have to see for ourselves," came the reply. "Take your walking sticks, as I hear that it is a very steep climb to the top of the falls."

Sue skipped outside and was bouncing her ball when the others joined her. Then, tapping their walking sticks against the sidewalk, the family set off along the street.

They had passed the town hall with its tall clock tower and were on their way up a steep hill when Pete suddenly remembered that he had left his wallet on the dresser in the hotel room.

"Don't worry about it," Ricky said. "We locked our door."

Just then the children saw a sign, *Triberg Wasserfall*. They wound along a wooded path beside a rocky ravine. A stream leaped between its steep banks.

"I hear the falls!" Ricky cried out as he ran ahead.

Suddenly the cataract came into view. The silver thread of water came down the mountainside in giant steps. At the foot of each falls was a pool of water, which overflowed to the one below until the cascade reached bottom.

"Let's climb to the top!" Ricky called out and started up the trail. Other visitors smiled at the youngsters as they trudged slowly toward the summit of the waterfall.

Even though Sue used her little cane, her short, chubby legs could not keep up with the others, so Pam held her hand. As the little girl toiled up the hill, the rubber ball began to work its way out of her dress pocket. Finally it fell to the ground and rolled into the ravine. Quick as a mouse, the child jerked away from her sister and scrambled after the ball.

"Come back, Sue!" Pam cried out and tried to catch her.

Half-sitting, Sue slid down the steep bank to the water's edge where the ball was lodged against a stone. The other children looked on, aghast, as the little girl reached over gingerly and retrieved the toy. She put it in her pocket, then tried to climb back up the slope, but every time she took a step, she slid backward.

"Hold on there! I'll get you!" Pete called out. Using his walking stick as a brake, he inched his way down the ravine toward his little sister, but the earth was crumbling beneath his feet.

Hang on!

"Crickets," he thought, "if I go down any farther, I won't be able to get back up."

Pete extended the crook handle of his cane, but the child's short arms could not reach it. "Hook your cane handle to mine," he called, "and hang on." The little girl did as he instructed and, pulling gently, he hauled her up to him.

The boy turned about to find Pam extending her cane in his direction, and, with Holly and Ricky's help, Pete and Sue were pulled up the slope.

"Whew—thanks!" Pete said when they were back on the trail.

The children's parents, who had gone on ahead of them, hastily returned when they saw what had happened. Mr. Hollister took Sue up on his shoulders and they trudged to the summit of the falls where a wooden bridge crossed the foaming water.

"Oh, what a beautiful sight!" Pam said, as she looked down at the silver threads of water bouncing off the rocks.

After Pete had taken pictures and the climbers had rested, they started the long descent. Upon reaching the bottom of the falls, Mr. Hollister set Sue on the ground once again. With their canes tapping merrily on the sidewalk, the family returned to the hotel.

Near the entrance, Holly stopped when she heard a meowing. Glancing about she saw a half-grown calico cat mincing her way along the sidewalk. Holly picked up the kitten and carried her inside the hotel. "Look what I found, Mommy," she said, putting the cat down on the lobby carpet. Instantly the little creature stood on her hind legs and pawed at the air.

"Goodness," Mrs. Hollister said, "it looks like a trick cat."

"What will we call her?" Ricky asked.

"Katze, of course," said Pam.

"But she's not ours," their mother said. "You must return her to her owner."

Just then Mr. Mueller came by and glanced at Katze. "So, you are looking for your master," he said, and, turning to the others, he added, "This cat belongs to Mr. Fritz. He has trained her. Do you have a ball?"

Sue pulled hers from her pocket.

"Bounce it," Mr. Mueller said. As Sue did this, Katze stood on her hind legs and caught the ball in her forepaws.

"Yikes! A cat baseball player!" Ricky cried out. "Can she swing a bat, too?"

"No, I'm afraid not." Mr. Mueller chuckled. "She's only a catcher."

The hotel proprietor said that the kitten sometimes wandered away from the alley behind the red door.

The children perked up their ears in curiosity.

"What red door?" Pete asked.

"You'll see tomorrow when you visit Mr. Fritz," the man replied with a wink.

"May we keep Katze tonight?" Holly asked.

Mr. Mueller said that they might have the calico cat as their guest. "The maid will bring a box to your room," he said, "and the kitten can sleep there."

After promising to get a saucer of milk for the cat, Mr. Mueller excused himself and the Hollisters trooped upstairs, with Holly holding Katze over her left shoulder. Ricky went with the girls to play with the cat.

As Pete entered his room, he was startled to see a man's head disappear below the window ledge. At first the boy was too stunned to move. He glanced at the dresser where he had left his wallet that morning. It was gone!

Pete ran to the window and looked down to see a man descending the fire escape. All the boy could see was that the fellow was tall with narrow shoulders and a bald spot on top of his head.

"I'll head him off," Pete thought and dashed out the door and down the stairs. He raced through the empty lobby and around the front of the hotel to the side garden directly below his window. No one was in sight. The stranger had vanished!

CHAPTER 12

The Schnitzelmeister

FRANTICALLY Pete searched about the garden but could find no trace of the intruder. As the boy hurried back inside the hotel, he saw that Mr. Mueller was now behind the desk.

The proprietor hailed him. "You were looking for this, I'll bet," he said and held up Pete's missing wallet. "I found it on the floor of the lobby just now when I came in."

Astonished, the boy took his property and told the hotel man what had happened.

"I know what that scoundrel must have done," Mr. Mueller declared. "He re-entered the hotel through a first floor window and walked down the stairs after seeing you run out. Then, after dropping your wallet in the lobby, he made his escape into the street. I suppose the money has been removed."

Quickly Pete looked through it. His identification card, pictures of the family and some German coins were still there. But the cuckoo clock note was missing!

"Oh!" the boy exclaimed. "They finally got it." A look of despair came over his face. Mr. Wetter and

112

his henchmen now had the strange message, and the race to solve the mystery was on even terms. "If there's a treasure, they may find it before we do," he thought.

Pete ran upstairs to tell the rest of the family what had happened. "We must report this to the local police immediately," Mrs. Hollister said, and her husband agreed.

Pete and his father set off for the police station, where they discussed the problem with a young lieutenant.

"I'm sorry," the officer said, "that visitors should be treated this way. Do you know what the note said?"

When Pete repeated the odd message that Mr. Elser had translated, the man shook his head. "Those are directions, no doubt, but where is the starting point?"

"Perhaps the thief knows," Pete said, "and he will beat us to the prize."

"You may come to me for help if you need it," the officer said. "Meanwhile, I'm afraid I can do nothing further for you."

As Pete and his father walked back to the hotel, the boy looked worried. "I hope Mr. Fritz can help us solve this riddle when we meet him tomorrow," he said.

The family was up at daybreak next morning and waiting outside the hotel dining room even before it had opened for breakfast.

"You are early birds," said Mr. Mueller, beaming, as he showed them to a table.

When the food came the children pitched in promptly.

"Please don't eat so fast," Mrs. Hollister said to Ricky. "There is no hurry."

"But we have to go see the wood carver right away," the redhead replied.

The other children agreed and Pete added, "Every minute counts now, Mother."

"But Herr Fritz may not be up so early," came the reply.

As the children's faces fell, the voice of the proprietor came from behind them.

"Excuse me, Frau Hollister, I could not help overhearing. *Der Alte* Fritz is a very early riser."

"Then may we go right away, please, Mother?" Pam asked.

Mrs. Hollister hesitated. "Daddy and I planned to write some letters first thing this morning."

"We could go by ourselves," Pete suggested quickly.

"I'm sure it would be all right," Mr. Mueller put in. "The old man welcomes children."

"Very well," Mrs. Hollister said. "But please be back here in an hour."

Quickly the youngsters finished eating and Pam wiped off Sue's milk mustache while Holly excused herself to get Katze.

When the pigtailed girl returned with the cat,

Mr. Mueller accompanied the children to the front entrance and pointed down the street on the opposite side. "The red door is in the middle of the block," he said. "Just open it and go in."

Among the little shops along the avenue were doors of various colors. The Hollisters crossed the street. They passed a blue one and close to it was a dark maroon door.

"This is the one, I bet," Ricky said.

"But it isn't red," Pam protested.

"Maroon's about the same," Ricky declared. "I'm sure this is the one Mr. Mueller meant."

Before the others could stop him, the boy turned the knob, opened the door and walked in.

Much to his surprise he found himself in someone's living room. There was a fireplace along one side, a table in the center and a rocking chair near a far window in which sat an old lady wrapped in a heavy, fringed shawl. She was rocking back and forth. When she saw Ricky she gave a wide smile, said something in German and beckoned to the boy.

"Oh, excuse me! I—I'm not who you think I am," Ricky stammered. "I'm someone else. I'm sorry, lady. Good-by." Ricky backed out quickly, and noting his red face, the others smiled.

"What did you see?" Pam asked.

"There was an old lady in a rocking chair," Ricky replied, "and she wanted to talk to me, only I don't speak German."

"Maybe she needed some help," Pam said. "Don't you think you ought to find out?"

"Not me," Ricky declared. "You go."

The warmhearted girl stepped to the maroon door and opened it. The woman was still rocking. She beckoned to Pam and the girl went over to her. The old lady's face was wrinkled but she had kind eyes and a pleasant smile.

"Do not be afraid," she said in slow English. "Every day my door is opened at least once by someone looking for Karl Fritz."

Pam laughed and said, "We're looking for him too. I'm sorry my brother made the mistake."

The old lady smiled. "You are Americans, aren't you? I went to the United States once, and I am especially happy to see children from there." Her eyes twinkled. "When a girl or boy comes to my door by mistake, I always have a surprise." She took the cover off a wicker sewing basket by the side of her chair, pulled out a bag and shook some gumdrops into Pam's hand.

"Thank you," the girl said.

"Come back and see me again," the old lady called to Pam as she stepped out of the maroon door.

"See, Ricky, you didn't wait for the surprise," Pam teased her younger brother. Then she shared the candy with the others and they all chewed on gumdrops as they continued their search.

In a few minutes they came to a bright red door

Katze leaped from Holly's arms.

with a brass knob. Pete turned it and stepped over the threshold into a long alley.

At the far end was a narrow, two-story house with a peaked roof. As the children walked toward it, they came to a courtyard on their left where six cats sat sleepily in the sunshine. Katze meowed, leaped from Holly's arms and purred her way to the largest of the cats.

"That's her mother, I bet," the pigtailed girl remarked as they continued down the passageway.

When they reached the house they saw a small door on their left. Over it hung a sign, *Karl Fritz, Schnitzelmeister*.

Pam tapped lightly on the door. It was opened by a young man who wore a white shirt open at the neck with the sleeves rolled up. Over it he had a long, green apron.

"Is Mr. Fritz here?" Pam asked.

"Come in, please," the youth said.

As the children stepped inside, they were greeted by the loud ticking of rows of cuckoo clocks which hung along one wall. The young man pointed across the room to a workbench where a small, round-faced man sat carving a block of wood. He looked up at the children and his face crinkled in a happy smile.

Pete introduced himself and the others to the wood carver.

"So you come from America?" he asked in halting English. "I am honored by your visit."

118

The wood carver introduced his apprentice, Hans, who said that many people came long distances to visit *Der Alte* Fritz. He explained that means "Old Mr. Fritz."

"But why do you wish to see me?" the wood carver asked quizzically.

"It's about a mystery," Pete replied.

While the *Schnitzelmeister* and his apprentice listened intently, the Hollisters took turns speaking slowly so that the Germans would understand. Pete explained how they had found the strange message in the cuckoo clock door. "Do you know who put it there, Mr. Fritz," he asked, "and what it means?"

The wood carver looked perplexed and shook his head. "I don't know," he said.

As the old man spoke, Pete noticed that Hans was backing slowly toward the door. Then all at once the clocks sprang to life as the tiny birds poked their heads out and began to cuckoo. Sue held her hands over her ears while Holly clapped her hands and laughed. After eight calls all the cuckoos disappeared, as if yanked back into their little houses by an unseen hand.

Pete turned his attention once more to Hans. The door stood open. The helper had slipped out!

CHAPTER 13

A Wooden Lion

WHEN they noticed that Hans, the apprentice, had suddenly disappeared, Pete and Pam exchanged knowing glances. While the younger children chatted with the wood carver, Pete drew his sister toward the back window of the shop, which looked down onto a foaming stream twelve feet below.

Out of earshot Pete whispered, "I'm suspicious of Hans."

"So am I," she replied. "He may be the one who put that note in the cuckoo clock door."

"He's probably making a getaway now," Pete said gloomily.

But when they turned back to join the conversation, their mouths fell open with surprise, for into the door came the helper. In his hands he held a stack of letters.

"Excuse me for leaving so suddenly," he said, "but you were so interested in talking that I did not wish to disturb you." Hans explained that mail arrived at the nearby post office at eight o'clock and he had gone down to get it.

"We have many letters from America," he said,

showing them the United States stamps. "Later I must take some clocks to be mailed."

Both Pete and Pam felt sheepish. Hans was not a suspect after all.

The apprentice went to one end of the workbench and began packing a clock into a wooden shipping box. While he worked, they all talked about the cuckoo mystery and went over each detail again. True, Mr. Hollister had ordered clocks and had received three. But why the message had been inserted in the door, and who had done it, was as much of a puzzle to the *Schnitzelmeister* as it was to his apprentice.

"If there is a golden cuckoo in Triberg I do not know about it," *Der Alte* Fritz went on. He told them that before the war several famous golden cuckoo clocks had been made, but since that time, none, so far as he knew.

"Perhaps the riddle refers to one of those old golden clocks," Pete suggested.

"Maybe," the wood carver agreed.

"Why would it be hidden now?" the apprentice wondered, and no one could answer him.

"But where is the clock which was stolen at the airport?" the wood carver asked.

"Yikes," said Ricky, "I forgot to bring it." He explained that it was in his luggage, and raced out of the shop to get it.

"I shall repair it for you," Mr. Fritz said with a broad smile. "And add a surprise of my own."

"Oh, what is it, Mr. Schnitzel?" Sue piped up.

Der Alte Fritz chuckled. "That you must wait and see," he replied.

"Speaking of *Schnitzel*," Pete said, "we have another mission in Germany." He told about the carved wooden lion that had been burned at Mr. Spencer's house in Crestwood. "We've come to you for another one because we understand that you are the best carver in all Germany."

The old man smiled, picked up a small, sharp knife and a block of wood and quickly made a tiny duck. "When you have been carving as long as I have," he said, giving the little figure to Sue, "you should be good at making birds and fish and lions, too."

He put down his tool and walked to the far end of the bench where a piece of canvas lay over something humpy. With a quick motion of his hand, Mr. Fritz removed the cover. There, beneath it, was a handsome, crouching lion.

"Oh, just what we want!" Pam cried out.

"He's the right size," Holly said.

"You like him, *ja?*" the wood carver asked, then added with a sad look, "but I am afraid the lion is not for sale."

"Is it for someone else?" Holly wanted to know.

Mr. Fritz pursed his lips and bobbed his head thoughtfully. "It is for me," he said. "All my life I have carved things for other people, but I want a lion for myself."

"Oh, just what we want!" Pam cried out.

"Can you make us another one like it?" Pete asked.

The wood carver said that would take a long time.

"I am old now," he added. "Maybe I could not even finish it."

The children looked sadly at the *Schnitzelmeister* and Pam said, "You will live long enough to make many fine lions, Mr. Fritz."

Hans spoke up and said he thought so, too. Then he added, "I have to go to the post office with these boxes. I hope to see you when I return."

After the apprentice had excused himself and gone off, the wood carver said, "My upstairs show-room you must see, too. More cuckoo clocks and other things I have carved. Come with me."

He opened the shop door and was about to lead them to a small outside stairway when a tall man came down the alley. He was almost bald and so thin that his cheeks appeared to be sucked in. Two heavy frown lines creased his forehead. The Hollisters could tell from his dress that he was not an American, and the wood carver spoke to him in German.

The man shook his head no, and went into Mr. Fritz's shop while the old man and his visitors ascended the stairway to the second floor. There they found a room as large as the one below. It was filled with cuckoo clocks and carvings.

"Most of these clocks will go to America," Mr.

Fritz said. There were several elves, a family in native costume and a blacksmith in his shop.

As Mr. Fritz showed these to the children, he suddenly paused and his eyes grew wide. "*Ja*, now I remember!" he said.

"Remember what?" Ricky asked.

The wood carver became excited and his hands moved quickly as he spoke. "Schmidt—Herr Schmidt worked in my shop two months ago. Perhaps he knows something about the mystery."

The wood carver said that he had been ill for several weeks. During this time a Mr. Schmidt from Hornberg had helped Hans to ship clocks to America.

"That's a wonderful lead," Pam said, her eyes sparkling with excitement.

"We know where Hornberg is," Pete offered.

"Good," came the reply. "Then maybe there you can find Schmidt and ask him of this mystery. I do not like that you have received so much trouble from my cuckoo clock."

They all went downstairs again into the workshop, but when they entered the tall stranger was not there.

Mr. Fritz shrugged. "Maybe he got tired of waiting. But if he wants to buy, he'll come back."

Just then Ricky arrived with the damaged clock under his arm and the cuckoo in his pocket. He gave them to the *Schnitzelmeister*.

"Please," Sue piped up, "Will you put the little bird back in his house?"

"*Ja*, I will fix this for you, and I promise you the surprise."

"And if you change your mind," Pete said, "we would like to purchase your wooden lion."

Their eyes went to the end of the bench where the carved animal had stood. The space was vacant!

"My lion! Where is my lion?" the wood carver exclaimed, glancing nervously about his shop.

"I know," Pete said. "That tall man who came in here must have stolen it!"

"I saw a tall man in the alley," Ricky said, "but he didn't have the lion with him."

While they were all looking around the shop, Hans returned. No, he had not taken the carving either.

Pam reasoned that the thief, whoever he was, certainly would not want to be seen walking through the streets of Triberg with a huge wooden lion.

"So he must have wrapped it up," Pete said.

But Hans examined the spool of paper on a small wrapping table. "This has not been used," he said. "Here is the uneven edge where I tore it off."

"How about the cord?" Pete asked the helper. "Has it been touched since you last handled it?"

"*Ja*," the apprentice replied after he had examined the heavy cord. "Someone has used this."

"Maybe the thief brought paper or a cloth with

him to wrap the lion," Pam said, "and then tied it up with this cord."

"But the tall man wasn't carrying anything," Ricky insisted.

The children looked at one another, baffled. Where could the lion have gone?

CHAPTER 14

A Friendly Deer

WHILE the children and Hans had been talking about the missing lion, the old wood carver had not said a word. Now Pam looked at the *Schnitzelmeister*. He sat dejected, with his chin on his chest.

"Don't worry, Mr. Fritz," Pam said kindly. "We'll help you get your carving back."

"I'll report the theft to the police," Pete declared.

"I'll go with you," Hans volunteered and they hurried from the shop.

"Such an impossible riddle," the old man said sadly. "First the lion was here and the stranger was here, now they are both gone, but the man didn't carry it away. How did the lion go? It didn't walk." He shook his head hopelessly.

"We carve things out of soap," Holly said, trying to cheer him.

"Could you show us how to make animals like ducks and dogs and baby lions?" Ricky added.

Herr Fritz brightened when he heard this. "*Ach, ja!*" he exclaimed, and his eyes twinkled. "Many children I have taught to be wood carvers. I'll give you a lesson tomorrow."

"If we can take time from our sleuthing," Pam

128

put in. "We mean to solve the cuckoo clock mystery."

"And now we must find the missing lion, too," Holly added.

"We'll all help," Ricky said stoutly.

"Let's go right away and look around the streets for that tall man," Pam suggested. "Even if he didn't take the lion, he might be able to tell us if anyone else took it."

"We will report back to you as soon as we find out something," Holly told the wood carver.

Sue thanked him for the tiny duck and the children hastened out of the shop and down the alley to the sidewalk. They looked into all the shops on both sides of the avenue, but there was no sign of the tall stranger.

"We've been gone almost an hour," Pam reminded them. "Mother and Daddy will be waiting for us at the hotel."

On the way back they met Pete. A few minutes later the children joined their parents in the lobby and related their early-morning adventure.

"So we've found a lion for Russ, only to lose it," Mr. Hollister remarked.

"Perhaps we can find it again, Daddy," Holly said.

"We had better stay here today and search for the tall man," Pete said.

His mother and father agreed.

"But what about going to see Mr. Schmidt in

Hornberg?" Pam asked. "That's a clue to the cuckoo clock mystery and we ought to follow it right away. There's no time to lose."

"Crickets!" exclaimed Pete suddenly. "Why didn't I think of it before! We can work on both mysteries right here. The tall man who took the note from my wallet may be the same one we saw in Mr. Fritz's shop this morning."

"He could have gone there to question Mr. Fritz about the mysterious message," Pam put in.

Everyone was excited by the idea and Pete suggested that they get a map of the town and divide it into three parts. "Mother and Sue and I can search for the man in one section, Daddy and Ricky in another, and Pam and Holly in the third."

The others were enthusiastic about the plan, and in a short time the three teams set out, agreeing to meet at the hotel again for supper.

Promptly at six o'clock Ricky and his father tramped into the lobby to find the other sleuths already sitting there. No one had seen the tall thief.

"We didn't get our man," Ricky said, "but I did bring back something." From his pocket he took a small mechanical mouse that had caught his eye in one of the shops.

"I bought something too," Holly said, and showed the others a little doll with yellow braids.

After the hungry family had eaten a good hot meal of roast, dumplings and thick brown gravy, Mrs. Hollister put Sue to bed. Holly and Ricky stayed in the hotel to play with their new toys, and Pete and Pam strolled to the edge of the cool woods near the waterfall.

"Why would anyone want to steal that big wooden lion?" Pam wondered.

"Because it's worth a lot of money," Pete replied. "Perhaps two or three hundred dollars."

The youngsters found a fallen tree near the edge of the stream which gurgled from the foot of the waterfall. Pete rested his chin on his hand and thought over what had happened that morning at the wood carver's shop. The tall man had been left alone with the lion and it had disappeared. But the stranger had walked away from the shop empty-handed!

As Pete looked into the churning water an idea suddenly struck him. He leaped to his feet. "Pam," he exclaimed, "I've got it! Remember what else beside the lion was missing from the shop?"

"Some cord."

"Right! And I think I know what the thief did! He tied the heavy cord about the lion, opened the shop window and lowered the carving out of it."

"This stream runs right behind the shop," Pam reminded him. "The lion might have fallen in it."

"The thief probably let the carving down only part way," Pete answered. "Then he shut the window tightly on the cord, hoping to let the lion dangle there until darkness."

"When he could come back without being seen," Pam said, "and get his loot."

"I think so," her brother said, adding that chances of anyone seeing the lion hanging in the back of the old building were not likely.

"Pete, it's starting to get dark now. What shall we do?"

"Go to the rear of the shop and see if the lion is still there!"

"Shall we call Dad first?" the girl asked.

Pete glanced at his watch. "I don't think there is time enough. Let's go. It's quite a distance!"

Fortunately the way was all downhill. The children alternated walking fast and trotting along the sidewalk until they came to the red door.

The cool of the evening came with the darkness, and Pete and Pam smelled the fresh scent of pines as they crept down the gloomy alley. The cats had gone. Pete led the way to their left, through the small courtyard, then down a slope to the back of the shop building, which bordered on the stream.

Pete hardly dared to look around the corner of the foundation. He put one eye to the edge of the stone and peered along the gray wall. The boy sucked in his breath at what he saw. There, dangling from beneath the window, was the wooden lion. And, reaching for it with upstretched hands, was the tall man!

Pete ducked back. "Pam, he's there! He's trying to get the lion!"

"Can we grab him?" the girl asked anxiously.

"If there is a tussle," Pete said, "we may all fall into the water. But I guess we'll have to risk it. Follow me!"

Just as Pete stepped onto the narrow ledge of land between the building and the rocky stream a light winked on in the window above them. Pete glanced up at the yellow pane. Perhaps the old wood carver had returned.

Pete cried out as loudly as he could. "Herr Fritz, open the window!"

The tall, thin man jerked his head to one side and saw the children. He spoke harshly in German, then, standing on tiptoes, tried to reach the lion again. His fingertips touched it and it swayed.

"Herr Fritz, do you hear me? Open the window!" the boy cried again.

There was a rustling sound from above and the sash was thrown up. Instantly the cord was released and the lion fell, hitting the tall man on the head. He staggered, swayed, lost his balance and fell into the cold water.

"Oh, he'll drown," Pam cried as the current carried him downstream. But the icy chill revived the groggy man. He made his way back to the riverbank several houses below, climbed out and, with a shrill cry at the Hollisters, disappeared among the houses.

"*Was geht da?*" Karl Fritz had been calling with his head poking out of the window above. Then

133

suddenly he recognized Pete and Pam. "What are you doing there? It is dangerous."

"We found your lion!" Pete shouted. "Wait a minute and we'll bring it up to you."

In the dim light the children could see the wooden animal lying face up inches from the edge of the churning water.

Even between them, the youngsters had all they could do to carry the heavy carving along the ledge of ground, up through the side yard and into the alley. There Herr Fritz met them and lugged his prized possession into the shop. The strong cord was still tied around it.

Pete was so excited that he had difficulty speaking slowly so that the old man could understand what had happened.

"You figured that out all by yourself?" the wood carver asked admiringly. "*Ach*, you are schmart, so young."

The *Schnitzelmeister* placed the lion on his workbench and looked at it fondly. Then he went on, "The thief got away. But he may return to harm you—even to take my lion again. I will sell it to your friend in America."

"Crickets, that's good!" Pete said, and Pam gave Herr Fritz a quick hug.

The wood carver told them that he would have Hans crate the lion next morning and send it to Mr. Spencer in Crestwood.

Pete and Pam raced through the red door and back to their hotel to report the good news.

"The man who got dunked," Ricky asked, "was he the same one we saw in the shop today?"

"He was tall enough," Pete replied, but had to admit that it was too dark to be sure.

"And now, my young detectives," said Mr. Hollister, "what are your plans for tomorrow?"

Pete suggested that they drive to Hornberg to question the fellow named Schmidt. He seemed to be the only one who might know something about the mysterious cuckoo clock message.

"But I want to see Mr. Schnitzel—I mean Fritz," Ricky said, "'cause I want to be a wood carver."

Holly said she would like to take a lesson, too, so it was agreed that the two youngsters would remain in Triberg with their father while Mrs. Hollister drove Pete, Pam and Sue to the neighboring town where Cliff Jager was staying with his grandparents.

"I am proud of you," Mrs. Hollister told the older pair. "One mission already has been accomplished. We have found a suitable lion."

"And we'll solve the other mystery, too," Pete said. "Thank you for helping us tomorrow, Mother."

Hornberg was not far from Triberg. Next morning Mrs. Hollister drove out of town and headed north. After they had traveled for a while, Pete asked his mother to stop by the roadside while he took a picture of a beautiful long valley which lay before them.

Just as they got out of the car, Sue exclaimed, "Oh, look over there—a deer!"

A small doe stood like a statue at the edge of the forest.

"Maybe it's the tame deer of the legend," the little girl said. She ran off quickly toward the animal, with Pete and Pam following her.

Sue turned about and called, "Look, Mother, it's not even moving. Come on, maybe we can pet it."

The Hollisters approached the doe closely, whereupon the beautiful creature turned and walked into the woods.

"Oh, I know it's the magic deer!" Sue said. "And he's leading us to the prince."

The doe walked along a well-marked trail to a clearing. There the family stopped in surprise. Before them a small castle stood atop a grassy knoll, and at the main gate a man beckoned toward the deer.

"See, I told you!" Sue cried delightedly.

"It does seem as if we are in a dream," Pam remarked as she watched the deer walk up to the man. He was dressed in knickers and wore a short green jacket. When the fawn approached, he bent down and stroked her head.

"Hello, Prince," Sue said, running up to him.

The man did not speak English well, but he gave

"Hello, Prince," Sue said.

the Hollisters to understand that he was the care-taker of the castle, and had several tame deer.

"And this one," Mrs. Hollister explained to Sue, "is probably a descendant of the deer in the legend."

Pete told the man that he was going to visit Cliff Jager, and the caretaker knew who the boy was. He said that Cliff was staying with his grandparents in the gray cottage on the first street of the town.

The Hollisters thanked him, returned to their car and drove off. It was nearly lunch time when Pete knocked on the door of the Jagers' house. Cliff himself answered it and, with a joyful shout, pumped his friend's hand.

"So you found me!" the boy said. "Come in, all of you, and meet my grandparents."

The elderly couple were cordial and invited the Hollisters to stay for lunch. They accepted, and when the meal was over Pete asked if they knew a man named Schmidt.

"Oh yes," Mr. Jager said. "You mean the Schmidt who worked in Triberg for a while? He used to help me in my bakery before I retired. I will tell you where he lives."

While Mrs. Hollister and Sue remained to talk with the grandparents, Pete, Pam and Cliff set off in search of the wood carver's former helper. As they approached the house where he boarded, a stooped man with a weather-beaten face came out. Cliff spoke to him in German and the man replied.

"This is Herr Schmidt," the boy told the Hollisters and introduced them.

"Ask him if he knows about the note in the cuckoo clock door," Pete said.

When Cliff translated this, Schmidt's eyes took on a wild, confused look.

"He does know about it!" the boy cried out.

Schmidt spoke rapidly and shook his head vigorously. Then Cliff said, "I can vouch for these people. They are friends of mine from America." Then he repeated the same thing in German. The man sat slowly on the front steps. He spoke to Cliff, but the Hollisters did not understand. Then the American boy said, "You were right about him, Pete and Pam. He says he does know about the mysterious message."

"But look," Pam said, "how frightened he is. He's trembling!"

CHAPTER 15

The Clock Tower

"WE'RE not going to hurt you," Pam said kindly. "Ask him why he is trembling, Cliff."

But the man refused to tell the reason. Then he pulled himself together and began to speak to Cliff, who translated for him.

Mr. Schmidt told the children that the clock with the mysterious message had been sent to America by mistake. As for the note—he suddenly broke off talking when he saw a short, husky man coming down the street. The fellow had a big nose and bushy black eyebrows.

"Schmidt!" the man called sharply and beckoned to him.

Schmidt looked more frightened than ever, and went to the stranger. The two conversed aside in low voices.

When the fellow left, Schmidt would not say another word to Cliff. Instead he waved the children off and hurried down the street. The young detectives ran after him.

"Please tell us more," Pam begged. "It is so important to us."

Finally the frightened man stopped and glanced back over his shoulder. The stocky fellow was out of sight. With Cliff quickly interpreting, Schmidt said, "All right, I'll tell you a little more, but please go when I do."

He told them that it was he who had put the message in the cuckoo clock. "I found the note in the house next to the clock tower in Triberg," he said. "Now let me alone." Before they could reply, he walked swiftly away.

"*Danke*, Herr Schmidt," Pam called, but the man did not look back.

"And thanks to you, Cliff," Pete said. "At least we have a clue to work on."

"Do you think Schmidt is mixed up in something dishonest?" Cliff asked as the children hastened toward his grandparents' house.

When they were almost there the husky man stepped out from an alley and accosted them.

"I know who you are!" he said, pointing a finger at Pete and Pam. "You're the Hollisters. I warn you —mind your own business."

"But—" Pete began in amazement.

"You are in danger," the man said threateningly.

"Who are you?" Pam asked, frightened by the stranger's behavior.

With a smirk, the man made a mock bow and said, "Call me Mr. X. And carry my warning back to your parents."

When he had disappeared down the street, the

three children hurried to the Jagers' home. After they had told their story, Mrs. Hollister was alarmed.

"This is terrible," she said.

"He seemed like a mean fellow, too," Pete remarked.

Cliff then questioned his grandparents about Mr. Schmidt. So far as they knew, he was an honest man. They were surprised to hear that he was acquainted with such a rude person as Mr. X.

"We'd better get back to Triberg as fast as we can," Pete suggested. "If Schmidt found that note in the house next to the clock tower, we should investigate there right away."

Although Cliff wanted them to stay longer, the Hollisters excused themselves, returned to their car and drove back to Triberg.

Mrs. Hollister parked at the hotel. Inside at the desk they learned that Holly and Ricky were out for an afternoon stroll with their father.

"We'd better not wait for them," Pete said. "Pam and I want to go to the house by the clock tower now."

"Sue and I will go with you," Mrs. Hollister said. "After the warning you had today, it is not wise for you to go alone."

The children and their mother hastened through the streets to the old clock tower, where they stopped and looked about.

Next to the ancient building there was only one

"I'll stay on guard out here with Sue," Mrs. Hollister said.

dwelling—a tall, narrow house. Beside it stood a one-story shop.

Tourists and townspeople who passed by took no notice of the four. After waiting and watching for a while, they decided that they were not being spied upon by the tall man, Mr. X or Mr. Wetter.

"I'll stay on guard out here with Sue," Mrs. Hollister said, "while you two go into the house."

Pete and Pam mounted a flight of stone steps and knocked on the door. It was opened by a gray-haired woman who wore a dust cap and held a broom in her hands.

"Do you know a man named Schmidt?" Pete asked her politely.

"I do not understand well," the woman said. "Do you speak German?"

Pam told her that they spoke only English, and the woman replied, "Speak slowly, and maybe I understand you."

She ushered them into her parlor and motioned to the sofa where they seated themselves. The woman untied her apron, put down her broom and pulled up a chair.

"I am Frau Gruber," she said. "Now tell me what you want."

Pete wished that they could get their ideas across to the woman more rapidly, while Pam was patiently explaining exactly who they were and why they were calling on her. They were not sure the woman understood the whole story, but this time she caught the name Schmidt.

"You mean the man from Hornberg?" she asked.

"Yes, that's the one," Pete replied. "Do you know him?"

The landlady stared at the wall as if she were looking far into the past, then she said, "Yes, Herr Schmidt had a room here, but that was long ago."

The children looked surprised. "How many years?" Pete asked.

Frau Gruber sighed. "That is hard to remember. Sometime after the war. It was while he was looking for Peter Freuling."

"Peter Freuling," the boy repeated. "Who was he?"

Now the woman seemed impatient. She shrugged and stood up. "So many questions are hard for my brain."

"Oh please don't make us go yet," Pam pleaded. "Someone in this house gave Mr. Schmidt a very important note and we've got to find out who."

"Perhaps if we could see Mr. Schmidt's room," Pete said, "it might help us."

Frau Gruber looked at the eager youngsters and her face softened. "Come with me," she said.

Pete and Pam climbed the carpeted stairs behind the woman. She led them to one landing, then to another, finally arriving at the top floor of her house. "*Ja*, roomers keep me busy," she said, "but something I can do for children is all right."

The landlady walked along a short hall, inserted a key in a lock and opened the door. The room was small and tidy, with a bed, chest of drawers, a small table and chair.

"This is where Herr Schmidt lived when he stayed in my house." The children glanced around but could see nothing in the room that might supply a clue.

"What about Peter Freuling?" Pete pressed. "Did he live here too?"

The landlady shook her head. "Peter Freuling I have never seen."

"But do you know where he lives?" Pam asked. She hoped that perhaps he might be able to throw light on the cuckoo clock mystery.

"That man Freuling was last heard from in Berlin," the woman said.

The landlady seemed weary of her interrogation as she slipped a hairpin into the bun she wore on the back of her head.

But the children were far from weary. Their faces grew pink with excitement as Pam said, "Who was Peter Freuling? What did he do? Did he have a golden cuckoo clock?"

The landlady said, "You came here to ask about Schmidt and now you want to know all about Freuling. Well, I will tell you," she went on in a kinder tone. "Peter Freuling was a brother of Andreas Freuling, who lived in this very room and died here."

146

"Oh, that's too bad," Pam said. "When did it happen?"

"About a year after the war was over." Then Frau Gruber continued slowly, "Schmidt was the next tenant. He lived in this room after Andreas died."

Pete looked thoroughly perplexed and said, "Why did Schmidt want to find Peter Freuling?"

"He had a message for Peter," the woman said.

Pete and Pam exchanged a look of excitement. "What kind of message?" Pete asked.

"All I know is that Herr Schmidt found a little piece of paper in this room right after he moved in," Frau Gruber assured them. "It was sticking up here." She moved the desk and behind it showed them a space between the baseboard and the wall.

"The note could have fallen off the desk into that crack," Pam said.

"Andreas must have meant to send the message to someone," Pete reasoned. "Perhaps he got sick before he could address and mail it."

The landlady nodded. "Herr Schmidt said the note should go to Andreas' family. I told him about the brother, Peter, and Herr Schmidt searched hard for him. He wrote letters and asked everybody if they had heard of the man."

"Did he find Peter Freuling?" Pete asked.

The landlady gave a little laugh, shrugged her shoulders and said, "*Ich weiss nicht*—I don't know."

CHAPTER 16

Unlocking a Riddle

CLUES—clues—clues! Pete and Pam now had a hatful. They thanked Frau Gruber and hastened outside to Mrs. Hollister and Sue. Recounting what they had learned, they hurried back to the hotel, where they found the rest of the family waiting.

The children sat cross-legged on the floor of their parents' room, with the door closed so no one could hear, and Pete and Pam told again what had happened.

In summing up, Pete said, "We know Andreas Freuling started the whole mystery when he hid the message which Mr. Schmidt found and tried to deliver to Peter Freuling in Berlin."

"Was that the hocus-pocus about three o'clock and six o'clock and all that?" Ricky asked.

Pete agreed that it probably was.

Holly piped up, "And Mr. Schmidt never found Peter?"

Pam shook her head and said, "Mrs. Gruber didn't know."

"But why was the note in the cuckoo clock door?" Ricky asked.

"That's something we have to find out," Pam said.

"And also we have to learn exactly what the riddle means," Pete added.

All of them agreed that the coded message gave directions to some sort of treasure.

"But where should we start from?" Mr. Hollister questioned.

"I know!" Pam exclaimed. "If Andreas Freuling lived next to the clock tower, perhaps that was the starting point in his set of clues."

"Pam, I believe you have a good idea," Pete said. "Let's go to the top of the clock tower."

"It is probably too late today," Mrs. Hollister said. "Why don't you ask Mr. Mueller when visitors may go?"

Pete ran downstairs to talk with the proprietor. The hotel man knew the custodian of the ancient building and telephoned him.

"He will be able to take you up into the tower tomorrow morning at nine o'clock," Mr. Mueller said.

Pete thanked him and hurried back upstairs. It was decided that he and Pam should make the trip. Before they went to bed that evening, they recited the mysterious riddle over and over, just so they would not forget it.

Promptly at nine o'clock next morning Pete and Pam met the custodian at the foot of the clock tower. After introducing themselves, they followed the man up several flights of narrow stone steps.

When they reached the top, Pete exclaimed, "Crickets, look at all those wheels and things!"

The children could see the inner machinery of the clock whose face was visible outside the tower.

"Do you want to learn how the clock works?" the custodian asked them.

Pete said no, they would like to look at the view.

"It is not much," the man said, pointing to a narrow slit in the wall. "This is the only place to look out."

Pete felt his heart pounding with excitement. Had Andreas Freuling discovered this spot? Had he based his cryptic clues on the scene that the boy was about to see?

Pete stood on tiptoe and looked out of the opening. Close beside him, Pam whispered, "At three o'clock the hour hand points horizontally. What do you see?"

"Crickets, the waterfall! The riddle is starting to make sense, Pam!"

The brother and sister held a whispered consultation while the custodian took a large oilcan from a niche and lubricated the wheels inside the big clock.

"Six o'clock to the chimney pot!" Pam quoted. "At that time the hour hand should be perpendicular to your line of sight. What would it point to, Pete?"

The boy looked toward the waterfall again.

"What do you see?"

"There is an old house," he reported, "but it has no chimney pot."

"Oh dear," Pam said, "that's where our clues end."

Her brother replied, "Maybe not. We'll go to the place. Perhaps another good clue will show up there."

The children thanked the custodian, who led them down the stone steps. Just as they reached the sidewalk, Pam seized her brother's arm and pointed down the street. "Pete, those two men—they're spying on us!"

Pete wheeled about to see not only the tall man who had stolen the lion, but also the unpleasant stranger who had warned them in Hornberg.

The husky man started toward them, glowering, but the thin one grabbed his arm and whispered something to him. Then they hurried off in opposite directions.

"What do you suppose they're up to?" Pam asked uneasily.

"They have the coded message," Pete said, "and may have guessed the clock tower is the starting point. We'd better hurry to the old house near the waterfall."

"But," Pam objected, "they may be just waiting for us to lead them on the next step in the riddle. If we go to the hotel, that'll throw them off."

"Crickets," Pete said, "you're right."

He and Pam hurried back and told the others what had happened.

"Those men must be desperate to find the treasure," Mr. Hollister said gravely.

"We must give them the slip somehow," Pete said.

"I have an idea," Ricky spoke up. "If Mother and Daddy and Holly and I go off on a false search, maybe the men will follow us. Then Pete and Pam can go to the old house and look for clues."

"Crickets, that's a great idea!" Pete exclaimed.

With a great show of laughter and swinging their canes, the five Hollisters left the hotel and started down the street. In order to look suspicious they glanced into alleyways, peered up at second-floor windows, and seemed to be on a great search.

"Psst!" Holly said finally. "Don't look now, but I think the tall man is following us just as Ricky said he would."

Pete and Pam, meanwhile, slipped out the back entrance of the hotel and hurried off to find the old house they had seen from the clock tower. It lay on the far side of town, across the bridge that spanned the stream and near the foot of the waterfall.

"It must be the right place," Pam said, "because there are no other buildings around it."

"But it has no chimney pot," Pete reminded her, "so don't let your hopes go too high."

They walked up to the door and knocked. A plump little man answered. He had been a sailor in his day, he told the children, and had learned how to speak English. His name was Klar.

Pete explained what they were looking for. "Did this place ever have a chimney pot?" the boy asked.

"Yes," Mr. Klar replied, "but it was old and fell apart, so I took it down." Then he pointed to a small flue on the side of the house. "That is where the smoke comes out now," he said.

"Pam, we're on the right track!" Pete said, trying hard to hide his excitement.

"May we go inside your house and look around?" Pam asked. "We think an old treasure is hidden here."

The man chuckled. "Old, squeaky boards, yes, but treasure—I doubt that. You can come and look anyhow."

Inside, Pete found the chimney place.

"Nine o'clock to the wooden stair," Pam quoted softly. She put her arm out straight to the left, and it pointed to a closed door.

She and Pete hurried over and opened it. In a small hallway was a steep wooden stair.

"Now," said Pete, "twelve o'clock is straight up."

They glanced up the stairway to the second floor and could hardly believe their eyes. A trap door was neatly outlined on the ceiling.

"What's up there?" Pete asked Mr. Klar, who had followed them.

"A small attic room," he replied. "But it hasn't been opened in years. When I bought this place shortly after the war I peeked up there once, but saw the space was too small to use for anything."

"May we examine it anyway?" Pete asked.

"If you would like to," the man answered with an amused look.

He went away and returned shortly with a stepladder. The children helped him carry it up the stairs.

On the landing, the man unfolded the legs and said, "Do you want to go up? Just push on the trap door; it will open."

Pete climbed the ladder. At the top he reached up slowly until his hands touched the wooden square in the ceiling. He pushed, but it stuck. Then Pete gave a hard shove.

Creak! The door opened and a small cloud of dust fell on the boy's head. Pete choked and sneezed.

"You see what I mean?" Mr. Klar said. "It's been shut for years."

Pete poked his head up inside the hole and looked around. It was pitch black. The boy extended his arm and felt about the small enclosure.

Suddenly his fingers touched something. Pulling it toward him, he saw it was a heavy cardboard box. As he lifted it out of the hole, more dust fell on his head. He sneezed, nearly dropping the carton, but caught it in time. Holding his discovery under one arm, Pete let the trap door down easily, then descended the ladder.

"I think we've found it, Pam!" he said jubilantly as the householder shook his head in amazement.

Pam's eyes danced with excitement and she could hardly wait for her brother to open the box. Pete put it on the floor and lifted the lid.

Inside was an object wrapped in heavy flannel. Pete took it out and removed the covering.

It was an exquisite golden cuckoo clock! How the birds and leaves shone! On the base of it was a small sign that stated Leipzig Museum.

"Oh," Pam whispered, "isn't it beautiful?"

"How did you know it was here?" the man asked.

"I'm sorry, but that would take too long to tell you now," Pete said. "We must turn this cuckoo clock over to the police."

"*Ja*," the man agreed, "I do not own it." He looked at them, puzzled. "And certainly this is not the Leipzig Museum!"

The children replaced the clock in its box and, thanking Mr. Klar, hurried downstairs.

"I will go with you," the man said, "so I can find out all about this."

Carrying the precious carton in one arm, Pete hastened out the door, followed by Pam and the householder.

On the sidewalk, Mister X awaited them. Pete cried out as the stocky man snatched the cuckoo clock from him. He pushed the boy to the ground, ran to a waiting auto and sped off.

CHAPTER 17

Ricky's Hunch

"WE must get that man!" Pete cried out as he scrambled to his feet. "He's stolen the golden cuckoo clock!"

"*Ja*, we must go to the police at once!" the householder exclaimed. The children and he hurried off to the police station.

Excitedly the trio told their story to the same young lieutenant Pete had seen when he had reported the theft of the wallet and the lion.

Pam gave the officer a detailed description of the stocky thief. The policeman immediately sent two of his men out to look for the fugitive.

"Don't feel bad," the officer said to the children. "You can be proud of figuring out those mysterious directions in the note."

"Please, somebody tell me what this is all about," pleaded Mr. Klar.

While the officer explained to the puzzled man, Pete and Pam returned to the hotel.

They found the rest of the family in their parents' room, gaily chatting about how they had lured the tall, thin man in the wrong direction. "But it didn't work, Daddy," said Pam nearly in tears.

"We led the other fellow right to the house where the golden cuckoo clock was hidden," Pete said bitterly, "and he snatched it out of our hands."

Disappointed, the family listened to all that happened.

"But we won't give up!" Ricky said, throwing out his chest. "We'll chase that man and get the clock back again."

Trying to keep their hopes up, the Hollisters went downstairs for lunch, but the two older children ate little.

As they came out of the dining room they were startled to see the police lieutenant walk into the lobby. He told them that Pam's detailed description of the thief had been so accurate that the fellow had been identified in a short time. "He uses the name Herman Gotch," the officer said, "and lived in a small hotel on the hillside in back of this place. He shared his quarters with a companion, a tall fellow."

"The one who stole the message and the lion," Pete put in.

"They could have spied right into our room with binoculars," Ricky said. "I bet that's how the thief knew your wallet was on the dresser."

"That's likely," the officer replied. "Unfortunately both men left Triberg in a hurry a short time ago."

"Is there any chance of arresting them?" Mr. Hollister asked.

"We have one clue," the policeman replied. "I'll pass it on to you, in case you'd like to follow it." He told them that the manager of the small hotel where the suspect had stayed overheard the stocky man say that he was departing for Strasbourg."

"Why, that's in France," Mrs. Hollister remarked. "It's a large city on the Rhine River."

"Maybe he intends to sell the golden cuckoo there," Pam said.

"We will alert the police in Strasbourg," the officer said. "The men had two cars. Gotch left in one, carrying a small suitcase and a carton."

"He has the cuckoo clock then," Holly said.

The officer nodded. "His tall friend took the other car. Where he's headed, we don't know."

"Let's follow Gotch right away," Ricky suggested and the other children agreed eagerly.

"We'll catch the bad men for you," Sue said and patted the officer's hand.

The lieutenant chuckled and declared it would not surprise him. After pointing out the shortest route to Strasbourg on Mrs. Hollister's road map, he wished them luck and departed.

"Shall we continue on the cuckoo clock chase, Elaine?" Mr. Hollister asked his wife.

"Yes," she said, setting her chin.

"Hurray for mother!" Holly cried, bouncing up and down and clapping her hands. "She is brave!"

The children scurried up to their rooms and

hastily packed. Within half an hour the Hollisters had said good-by to Herr Mueller and were in the black Mercedes-Benz, heading toward the French border.

After an hour of driving toward the west, the deep, green valleys gave way to a broad plain. On either side of the road large farms stretched way into the distance and people in their yards waved to the Americans as they drove past.

Late in the afternoon the travelers came to a large bridge crossing the Rhine River. Arriving on the other side, they were met by a customs official, who checked their passports.

The customs man was a friendly young fellow in a blue uniform. His hat, which Pam thought looked like a round cheesebox with a short peak, gave him an official appearance.

As the officer was about to wave them through, Pam said, "Has a German by the name of Herman Gotch passed through here this afternoon?"

The customs man's face lighted. "I checked him through a few minutes ago," he said, then turning halfway, he pointed down the street. "There's his car now. That's Gotch. He's probably looking for directions." Then the man added, "Sorry to correct you, mademoiselle, but he is not a German."

Pam said thanks, and Mr. Hollister started the car quickly.

"Hurry—get him, Dad!" Ricky cried out.

"Not so fast," Mr. Hollister answered. "Let's trail him to find where he's going."

"You're a good detective," Pete praised his father, who now drove along slowly and stopped several car lengths behind the small auto in which the suspect was seated. The children could see that Gotch was studying a large map opened on his steering wheel.

"Oh," Pam said, as the small car started off slowly, "he must have the golden cuckoo with him. If we could only run out and get it!"

"Patience," Mrs. Hollister said, "we shan't let him get away this time."

Mr. Hollister followed the car until he lost sight of it in the heavy traffic. When he saw it again, it was parked beside a long dock on the waterfront. A gleaming white river boat was moored there.

"Daddy, he probably got on that boat," Pam said.

"We'll find out," her father replied, and parked his car behind the small one.

The vessel was long and broad and had two decks. A wide gangplank led from the dock onto the lower deck. Just as the Hollisters stepped out of their car and were about to cross the gangplank, Pam cried out, "Look! This is the *Eureka!*"

"The one Mr. Elser told us about?" asked Holly.

"Crickets!" Pete exploded. "If Gerhart Elser is the captain, he can help us capture Gotch."

With Mr. Hollister leading the way, the family

crossed the gangplank into a broad foyer. On one side was a small souvenir shop and beauty salon. Across from these were the porter's desk and captain's office. The door opened and a tall, well-built man in uniform stepped out. Seeing the questioning looks on the visitors' faces he said, "May I help you, please?"

"Are you Gerhart Elser?" Mr. Hollister asked.

The man looked surprised and said yes. When he was told the Hollisters were friends of his cousin Otto in America, he smiled happily and shook hands with each one of them.

"How did you know my boat was docked at Strasbourg for the night?" he asked.

The Hollisters admitted they had not known this. It was a lucky coincidence. "Maybe you can help us find the man we are looking for. We think he's one of your passengers," Pam said, and told the story about the suspect named Gotch.

Immediately the captain led them into his office and consulted his register. "Yes, he's aboard," the officer said, "and plans to debark at Düsseldorf."

After hearing the entire story about the cuckoo clock mystery, Gerhart Elser said, "Aha! I'll have his cabin searched. As captain, that is my privilege." He went off, and returned a short time later shaking his head. "The fellow has only a small suitcase," he said. "There is no package in his cabin."

"Was he there?" Pete asked.

"No," the captain replied.

"Maybe he's hiding the clock somewhere on the boat," Pete said.

"Why don't we call the Strasbourg police and have him arrested right now?" Ricky asked.

"Because they couldn't hold him unless he had the clock in his possession," Pete replied.

"That's right," the captain said. "I will have the steward and maid check carefully in every cabin for the golden cuckoo. If we do find it," he went on, "where shall we locate you Hollisters?"

"Let's ride down the river with Captain Elser," Holly suggested.

"That would be keen," Ricky said. "But what shall we do with the car, Daddy?"

Mr. Hollister explained that the rental agency could pick up the Mercedes-Benz at the dock. He looked questioningly at his wife and she nodded gravely. "We must find that clock," she said, "even if it means going all the way down the Rhine River on this boat."

"Good," Captain Elser replied. "I have accommodations for you. We sail in the morning."

While their baggage was transferred onto the river boat, Mr. Hollister arranged for the disposal of their rented car.

The three cabins assigned to the family were on the lower deck.

After Pete and Ricky had unpacked their suitcases, they stood at the window and looked out over the wide river.

"This is a great adventure," Pete declared.

"Yikes!" Ricky said, "I'm hungry."

The family was assigned to a seven o'clock sitting in the dining salon. A large round table had been arranged for them. What a surprise awaited them when they went in to supper! Occupying a small table nearby was Gotch himself. The fellow was lifting a tumbler of water to his lips when he saw the Hollisters. He nearly dropped the glass and choked on the drink.

While the others seated themselves, Mr. Hollister walked over and addressed the suspect.

"I want you to return that gold cuckoo," he said. "It doesn't belong to you, and you know it."

The man replied with a stream of words in German. His waiter, who was standing by his chair, translated: "I don't know you. I have never seen you and please don't bother me."

Mrs. Hollister shook her head when her husband returned to the table. "Gotch knows very well who you are and what you said. He's trying to make everyone think he does not speak English."

"We'll have to keep an eye on him," Pete said. "Now that he's seen us, he may try to leave the boat."

But Gotch remained in his cabin all evening. Pam was afraid he might escape during the night, so Mr. Hollister requested the captain to have the man watched.

Next morning, as the motor vessel was about to

set off down the Rhine, the officer informed them that Gotch was still aboard.

Satisfied that the fugitive could not get away until the next stop, the Hollisters lined the breezy rail and admired the beautiful Rhineland scenery. The river twisted and turned through lush green countryside. Many of the hills they passed were topped with ancient castles.

During the ride Pete and Pam learned that they would reach Düsseldorf, where Gotch was to get off, at four o'clock the following afternoon. But first there was to be an overnight stop at Rüdesheim. As they neared the city late in the day, the children saw that the hills were covered with vineyards. The even rows of grape arbors extended from the river clear to the top of the slopes.

"How neat they are kept!" Pam exclaimed as she admired the beautiful view.

Captain Elser turned his boat around in midstream, then, heading into the current, docked at the old city of Rüdesheim.

"We won't let Gotch out of our sight," Pete vowed, as the passengers left the vessel for sight-seeing.

Gotch marched off the gangplank with his head high. He had nothing in his hands, and did not go far. Pete, Pam, Ricky and Holly saw him as he strolled along the promenade by the waterfront. As the children went ashore Gotch glanced over his shoulder at them and frowned, but said nothing.

When he sat on a bench facing the river another man approached and sat down beside him. He was bald-headed with bristly gray mustache.

"That's the waiter at Gotch's table," Ricky whispered. "I wonder what they are saying."

The suspect got up hastily and strode back to the boat.

At once Ricky darted over to the waiter. "What did that man talk to you about?" he asked.

"*Das Wetter*," the waiter replied shortly. Then he got up and also returned to the *Eureka*.

Pete shrugged. "No luck there," he said when Ricky reported the conversation. "That fellow said they were talking about the weather."

"No, Pete," Ricky said. "I think they were talking about Mr. Donnerwetter."

Without waiting for the others, the redheaded boy dashed after the waiter. He tugged at his hand and said, "Were you talking about that bad man, Mr. Wetter?"

The waiter looked so startled that Pete and Pam suspected Ricky's hunch might be right.

The children returned to their parents on the boat.

"I bet Gotch and the waiter are in cahoots," Pete told his father.

"Now we have another suspect to watch," Holly said. But neither man did anything suspicious that evening.

By the time the children had awakened in the

166

"Were you talking about Mr. Wetter?"

morning, the boat once more was on its way down the Rhine. The beautiful farm country gave way to factories with big smokestacks. In the afternoon the large city of Düsseldorf came into view and the boat docked.

As the family hastened to the gangplank, Gotch approached carrying his suitcase. He turned to the Hollisters and with a bow said, "*Auf Wiedersehen.*" Then he walked off the boat.

"He doesn't have the golden cuckoo with him," Pete said. "That suitcase is too small. Maybe the waiter has it."

"Here he comes now," Pam exclaimed.

The bald-headed man strode swiftly down the gangplank, with a crate of lettuce on his shoulder.

"Wait!" Pete shouted and dashed forward. Ricky followed close on his heels.

The waiter turned around with a furtive look in his eyes. Pete and Ricky made a grab for him and he shoved the boys.

Splash! They fell into the Rhine River.

CHAPTER 18

Old Town Trap

"Save my brothers!" Sue called out as the boys bobbed to the surface, spluttering and coughing.

Instantly their father and Captain Elser seized life preservers and threw them into the water, because the stone wharf was too high for the boys to climb.

Pete and Ricky grabbed the rings, and were hauled, soaking wet, onto the gangplank.

"Did he get away?" was Pete's first question.

They all looked about, but the waiter was nowhere to be seen. Neither were Pam nor her mother.

Even though Ricky was dripping, Sue hugged him and said, "Mommy and Pam are chasing the bad man."

"Just as I thought," her father remarked, and added, "Hurry boys, change into dry clothes!"

While Pete and Ricky were dribbling water through the hallway on the way to their cabin, Mrs. Hollister and Pam were hurrying into the old part of town, which lay along the waterfront.

"There he goes! He still has the crate of lettuce,"

Pam said, as they spotted the fugitive rounding a corner.

"And I'm sure the golden cuckoo is in that box," her mother said. "Hurry, Pam!"

Mother and daughter followed the waiter, who was in so much of a rush he did not even turn around to see if he were being pursued. Suddenly he stopped before a restaurant, glanced up at the sign over the doorway and stepped inside.

"You keep watch in case he leaves, Mother," Pam said, "and I'll run back to get the others."

By the time she raced up the gangplank the two boys had changed into dry clothes and were on deck again.

"We found him!" Pam cried. "Come quickly."

Mr. Hollister scooped up Sue in his arms, Captain Elser hailed a waterfront policeman and they all followed Pam quickly through the streets to the restaurant.

"The waiter's still inside," Mrs. Hollister told them.

"I'll bet Gotch is in there too," Pete said.

The captain spoke rapidly to the policeman in German, then turned to the others. "I'll station myself at the back door," he said. "Mrs. Hollister, you had better fetch two more policemen in case we need them. The rest of you go in to identify the men."

Mrs. Hollister took Sue from her husband and hurried off, holding the little girl by the hand.

The children and their father followed the officer into the restaurant.

As it was early for supper, the place was nearly vacant. But in a dim, back corner sat four men around a table. When the policeman walked quickly up to them, they pushed back their chairs in fright. In the middle of the table stood the golden cuckoo clock.

The officer spoke sternly in German.

"There's Donnerwetter!" exclaimed Holly.

The stout man stood glowering between Gotch and the tall, thin man. Next to him was the waiter.

"Those Hollisters again!" Mr. Wetter cried out in anger. He seized the golden clock in his arms and made a dash for the back entrance.

Pete and Ricky were close on his heels when Captain Elser collared him in the doorway. Pete took the clock from the man and they marched him back to the table.

The policeman, meantime, had handcuffed Gotch to the waiter and Mr. Hollister had a firm grip on the tall, thin man.

Just then Mrs. Hollister, Sue and two other policemen hastened into the restaurant. The officers questioned the prisoners at length and when they had finished, turned to the Hollisters.

"This is a strange story," an English-speaking policeman said. "Did you really come all the way from America to catch these men?"

The Hollister children nodded while their parents

He made a dash for the back entrance.

smiled proudly. The officer declared they had done a great piece of detective work and related everything the men had confessed.

During the war, he told them, Andreas Freuling had found the clock in the ruins of the Leipzig Museum. He had fled the bombed city and taken the golden cuckoo with him for safekeeping. Sometime later, the thieves had heard of this and decided to steal it. By the time they managed to trace Andreas to Triberg, he had died. Schmidt had found the coded directions and was trying to locate Peter Freuling.

"And I'll bet his questions drew the gang's attention to him," Pete put in.

"Then," Pam reasoned, "when the thieves found Schmidt working in Mr. Fritz's wood-carving shop they tried to get the message from him."

"You're right," the policeman replied. "First, they offered to buy it, but when Schmidt refused, they threatened him. Convinced of the value of the paper, the man hid it in the cuckoo clock door.

"By mistake," he went on, "the clock had been sent to America. The crooks had wrung this information from Schmidt and forced him to give them a duplicate copy of the bill with the Hollisters' address on it. Then Wetter and Gotch flew to the United States in order to recover the note."

"Yikes!" Ricky said. "That old clock must be worth a lot."

"It's priceless," the captain spoke up. He told

them that the golden case had been made by one of Germany's most famous craftsmen. "The German people thank you for restoring it to them," he said.

Pete asked more questions and learned that the thieves had worked in shifts following the family. First Wetter had trailed them to the airport, while Gotch stole the two clocks from The Trading Post, just in case the note was in one of them. The stout man shadowed the Hollisters to Heidelberg, where he hired the pickpocket to snatch Pam's purse.

Then the thin man, whose name was Zorsky, had taken over, and when Gotch had returned from America, he joined him. In the meantime, Wetter had gone to Düsseldorf to make arrangements for selling the golden clock.

"How about the waiter?" Pete asked. "Is he one of the gang?"

"No," the officer replied. "Gotch bribed him to hide the clock and carry it off the boat."

Wetter spoke up bitterly in German.

The policeman translated. "He says that Zorsky was very foolish to steal the lion after the children had seen him in Fritz's shop. From there on the police had his description and were on the lookout for him."

"And now you are all caught and will be dealt with severely," Captain Elser said to the thieves.

"What will happen to the golden cuckoo clock?" Holly piped up.

"I will turn it over to the proper museum," said

the policeman, putting it under his arm. Once again he thanked the Hollisters, and the officers led the prisoners away.

"I guess this is as far as we go on your river boat," Mr. Hollister told the captain as they returned to the *Eureka*.

"It has been a pleasure," the captain said. "Please give my best regards to Cousin Otto."

The Hollisters stayed on board overnight and early next day rented a car to return to Triberg. There they were greeted warmly by Mr. Fritz, who was delighted when he heard the news of the capture.

"We will have a party tonight," the old wood carver said, "and there will be *singen* and *tanzen*."

"Singing and dancing," repeated Holly happily.

"And now," he added, "I will give you something so you do not forget your Black Forest adventure." He showed them their cuckoo clock hanging on the wall.

"I fixed it," he said, his eyes sparkling. "Watch!"

As the hour struck, the bird popped out saying, "Cuckoo!" The little figure's eyes lighted and blinked off and on! The Hollisters shouted with delight when they saw it.

"That's the secret I told you about," said Herr Fritz.

Suddenly Pam noticed that Ricky was looking quietly into space. "A penny for your thoughts," she said with a chuckle.

"I'm going to send a post card to Joey Brill," the red-haired boy said.

"What?" Pete hooted.

"Yikes!" Ricky replied, "if Joey hadn't broken the cuckoo clock door, we wouldn't have had this mystery."

"You're right," Pam said. "Send Joey a post card and say hello from all of us. Tell him he's—"

"Cuckoo! Cuckoo!" sang Sue's sweet little voice.

Cuckoo

German Folk-Tune

* Note: Play this accompaniment on piano.

Cuckoo, Cuckoo, ruf's aus dem Wald!
Lassen uns singen, tanzen und springen,
Cuckoo, Cuckoo, ruf's aus dem Wald!